A CASE OF
MURDER IN
MAYFAIR

A Freddy Pilkington-Soames Adventure Book 2

CLARA BENSON

MOUNT
STREET
PRESS

MOUNT STREET PRESS

Cover design by Shayne Rutherford at
wickedgoodbookcovers.com

Interior Design & Typesetting by Ampersand Book Interiors
ampersandbookinteriors.com

CHAPTER ONE

IT WAS A bright, brisk November day, the sort that shows off autumn at its finest. The afternoon sun shone low in the sky, glancing off the windows of the buildings, highlighting the trees in all their multi-coloured magnificence, and dazzling the eyes of the people hurrying about their daily business. A keen wind was blowing, cold, with a hint of frost to come, and the fallen leaves rattled as they skittered merrily along the ground, as though swept by the hand of an invisible giant. London looked pleasant in the sunshine—or this particular corner of London did, at any rate; the corner in which sat the Abingdon Hotel, that well-known haunt of royalty, statesmen, actors and other wealthy people of note. This elegant establishment, which occupied almost half a block in a quiet part of Mayfair not far from Bond Street, offered both luxury and discretion to those who could afford it, and was well used to the comings and goings of its guests at odd times, as well as their sometimes eccentric demands, which it prided itself on its ability to meet. In turn, its wealthy patrons appreciated the superabundance of amenities that were to be had therein, for behind the modest façade of red brick lay a degree of opulence and comfort of which the man in the street could only dream, but which the sort of clientèle the hotel attracted considered as the minimum necessary to make life at all bearable.

On this particular Tuesday, anyone passing by would have seen a little knot of people standing outside the Abingdon's grand entrance, chattering to one another with an air of suppressed excitement. The hotel's commissionaire, smart in his top hat and long coat with silver bands at the wrists, was watching them covertly while appearing not to, in case they decided—against all the rules of good manners and human decency—to rush him in a body and attempt to storm the place. He did not really expect this to happen, but he took his responsibilities very seriously, and was determined that no-one should ever say he had been caught napping. Indeed, the little crowd seemed quite content to stand patiently outside the hotel for as long as necessary. Occasionally, a motor-car would turn into the street, and they would all watch it eagerly as it drew towards them, then sigh and resume their conversations as it continued past without stopping. Several times had they been disappointed in this fashion, but they did not appear to be in any way discouraged, and looked set to stand there for the whole day if necessary.

Standing back from this group, lounging against a wall on the other side of the street in an attitude of supreme boredom, stood a young man. He wore a battered old Burberry with the buttons fastened up the wrong way and a crushed poppy in the lapel, which he had neglected to remove. His hat looked as though he had rammed it onto his head as an afterthought. A cigarette dangled from one corner of his mouth, and round his neck on a leather strap he carried a contraption that closer investigation revealed to be a folding camera. He had been there for some time, and was in no mood to appreciate the beauties of the day, for he had had little sleep and no lunch, and the cold wind was biting at his extremities most disagreeably. All he wanted was to get the job over and done with, then find the nearest eating-place that served hot meals and spend half an hour or so remedying his current deficiencies of comfort and nourishment.

He shifted his position and sighed, and at that moment noticed that he was being observed by an elderly man whose eccentric attire and paucity of teeth pronounced him to be a vagrant. The tramp saw he had been spotted, and sidled up to the young man with a look of speculation in his eyes.

'Got a light, guv'nor?' he said.

The young man produced a match. The tramp waited expectantly, and the other sighed and dug out a cigarette, which he handed over.

'You're a gentleman,' said the tramp, drawing on the gasper with great satisfaction and a smacking of the lips. He gestured at the camera. 'What's all this then? You waiting for somebody?'

'Dorothy Dacres,' said Freddy Pilkington-Soames.

'Who's that, then?'

'She's an American film star who is known for her beauty, grace, charm and acting ability. I dare say she's a whiz at quadratic equations and does good works for the sick and needy, too.'

'Never heard of her,' said the tramp, and spat.

'Don't let her hear you say that,' said Freddy. 'That sort of talk is death to one of her type. They must be the name on everybody's lips or they consider their existence to be futile.'

'That so?' said the tramp. He puffed on the cigarette and ruminated briefly. 'I ain't never watched a moving picture except once,' he said. 'And I'm half-blind anyway, so I didn't see much of it. Is that why she's come? To make one of these pictures?'

'So the rumour has it. There's to be a big production of some famous play or other, and they're making it here in England, and everybody's been wondering who is going to play the leading rôle. The latest word is that it's going to be Dorothy Dacres, and I'm here to see if she'll tell us whether that's true.'

'All foolery if you ask me,' said the tramp. 'A lot of people running around, flapping their mouths and not saying anything. How are we supposed to know what's happening?'

'Oh, but this is to be a talking picture,' said Freddy. 'It's quite a different thing.'

'A talking picture? Get away with you,' said the tramp jocularly, in the manner of one who has been entreated to believe in the existence of winged horses.

'It's true. They're all the rage now, and rather good fun, too. Why—'

He was interrupted by a sudden outburst of excited chatter from the little crowd across the road, who had seen another car turn into the street. This time it looked as though it were the real thing, for as it approached the Abingdon it began to slow. Freddy opened his camera and joined the throng, as the car came to a halt outside the front entrance and the commissionaire sprang forward to do his duty. The crowd seemed suddenly to have grown in number, and had to be held back by two or three smartly-uniformed men who had just emerged from the hotel to assist.

The first person to alight from the car caused the crowd to emit a sigh in unison. He was a tall, handsome man of twenty-five or so, with expressive brown eyes and a boyish smile. This was Robert Kenrick, an English actor who had lately been mentioned as having received several offers from studios in Hollywood to make films for them. He waved at the watchers, then stooped to hand a woman out of the car. The crowd let out a cheer as they saw her, and she put her hand to her breast and blinked, then smiled shyly, as though astonished at such a welcome. Dorothy Dacres had arisen seemingly from nowhere to star in many of the most profitable films of the past few years, and was considered one of the leading actresses of the day. Her golden hair, classical beauty and brilliant smile were loved by the camera and the public alike. She had not made a picture in some time, however, and there were those who whispered that, at thirty-six, she was getting past the useful age, and that her time in the spotlight was coming to an end. Still, as she preened and waved at her adoring audience, nobody could have possibly imagined that she had any such worry on her mind, or that the end of her career was anything but a dim spot on the horizon.

It now became evident that the crowd consisted of more than just Miss Dacres' 'fans,' for one or two young men with notebooks had appeared as if from nowhere, and began to shout questions at her. Freddy recognized them as fellow-reporters from other publications. They were asking whether she had anything to say about her presumed rôle as the tragic wife Helen Harper in *For Every Yesterday*, the film that was expected to begin production shortly.

'I can't say anything at this time,' she said. 'But we expect to make an announcement soon.'

'What about the rumours of an engagement between you and Mr. Kenrick?' said one young man.

'Oh, that's nonsense,' said Dorothy Dacres, with a peal of laughter. 'Wherever did you hear such a thing? Why, Bob and I are merely good friends.'

Here she turned to touch Kenrick's arm and give him a flirtatious glance which did nothing to quell the speculation.

Freddy had been worming his way to the front of the crowd, and now held up the camera to take a picture. Miss Dacres gave him her best side.

'I heard that Augusta Laing is to play the part of Helen Harper,' said another reporter.

Dorothy Dacres' smile faltered, and for a second she looked exceedingly cross, just as the shutter on Freddy's camera clicked. The smile returned almost immediately.

'Well, you'll just have to wait and see,' she said, with a wag of the finger.

She and Kenrick signed an autograph or two, then turned and were bowed into the Abingdon by the commissionaire. The crowd waited until they were out of sight, then began to disperse. Freddy struggled with the camera, which did not seem to want to fold up again, and grimaced. He feared he had lost his moment.

'Wish I'd brought one,' said a reporter from the *News*, gazing enviously at the machine. 'But they sent me here in a hurry.'

'I think I fluffed the shot anyway,' said Freddy, prodding at the bellows, which had stuck.

'Tough luck,' said the other. 'She wasn't saying much, was she? I don't suppose you've got anything?'

'No. You?'

The *News* reporter shook his head.

'Oh, well,' he said. 'I suppose it'll be the usual puff from the studio again.'

They both looked up as another car arrived and two people got out. One of them was a young man with an air of great concentration about him. He brought out with him two or three heavy-looking cases, one of which he handed to the commissionaire with an admonishment to be careful with it.

'It's Seymour Cosgrove, the photographer,' said the *News* man. 'I wonder whether he's come to do some publicity shots for the film. That must mean they definitely have given her the part. Who's the other one?'

'No idea,' said Freddy.

Whoever he was, he was quite obviously American, given the style of his dress. Perhaps fifty years of age, he was short and powerfully built, with a crumpled face that gave him something of the appearance of a fighter. He strode in through the front door of the Abingdon without hesitation, followed by Seymour Cosgrove.

'I expect he's one of the film people,' said the *News* man. He glanced at his watch. 'Well, we didn't get much, but I'd better think of something if I'm to catch the early evening edition. 'I'd get a new camera if I were you,' he added. 'I think that one's on its last legs. Cheerio.'

And with that he was off. Freddy struggled with the camera a little while longer, and finally succeeded in shutting it up. He, too, had a story to write, but there were more important things to attend to first, for his stomach was grumbling. He could easily scribble something down while he was eating. He thrust his hands in his pockets and turned away from the cold wind, heading in search of warmth and sustenance.

CHAPTER TWO

IN DOROTHY DACRES' palatial suite on the top floor of the Abingdon, all was confusion as Seymour Cosgrove set up the scene for the photographs he was about to take. From the cases had emerged a mountain of photographic equipment, and Cosgrove was currently sitting on the floor in among it all, putting together a tripod. The suite was the best accommodation the Abingdon offered—although they no longer called it a suite, but had recently begun describing it as a penthouse, in order to move with the times—and was reserved for the hotel's most revered guests. It had three bedrooms and an enormous living-room, in which a baby grand piano stood in pride of place on a fur rug that must have been four inches thick, at least. Above the piano hung a glass and chromium-plated chandelier of such splendour that it quite took one's breath away. The walls and furnishings were of the latest style—all inlaid walnut and reflective surfaces, tasteful beiges and pastels, with here and there a daring marble statue or a potted palm. The fabrics were from Paris, and the paintings on the walls—depicting subjects that ranged from the angular and garish to the wholly incomprehensible—were the work of the most noted modern artists. The penthouse had not one, but two terraces, the largest of which led off the living-room and was big enough to entertain a hundred people. Of the tariff it is better not to speak, except to say that all inquiries of that nature were referred to the manager, who was the only one permitted to communicate the terms, and who did so in a hushed, discreet voice he kept precisely for that purpose. Miss Dacres herself was reclining on a magnificent sofa which was upholstered in a particular shade of grey that matched her eyes and contrasted beautifully with her dress in coral red. The whole tableau created a pleasing effect of which she was fully aware.

'Will this take long, darling?' she said to Seymour Cosgrove. 'I'm awfully tired.'

He looked about him, then jumped up and went across to the baby grand.

'I like this piano,' he said, running his hand over it with a frown. 'We can do it here. Just you, or you and Kenrick, with the piano and the chandelier. Dramatic, but not too posed.'

He picked up a photographic lamp and placed it to greater advantage, then studied it for a second and moved it a few inches to the left.

Robert Kenrick came in from outside. He had achieved fame only recently, and was still new enough to the game to be impressed by everything.

'I say, there are splendid views from the terrace,' he said.

'Are there?' said Dorothy, with the jaded air of one used to luxury. 'I haven't looked.'

'Oh, but you must. I could see the rooftops of all the buildings for miles around.'

'There's another terrace off my bedroom, facing the front,' she said. 'Go and see if there are still people waiting outside.'

He did so, and returned after a minute.

'No, it's all quiet now,' he said.

'Oh,' she said, disconcerted. 'I guess this cold weather puts people off. In Hollywood the fans will wait outside for hours.'

'I must say, I'm looking forward to seeing America,' said Kenrick. 'England's all very well, but if one wants to be *really* famous then Hollywood is where it's at.'

His enthusiasm and naïveté were quite disarming, and Miss Dacres laughed.

'You're ambitious and not a bit ashamed of it,' she said. 'I like that. Most of you Britishers like to pretend you're above all that kind of thing, but not you—you make no bones about it.'

'But why should I? I want to be famous and have lots of money. I don't see it's anything to be ashamed of. I say,' he went on, as a thought struck him. 'People aren't really saying we're engaged, are they? Why, we only met two weeks ago. Where did they get that idea?'

'Oh, I telephoned the newspapers and told them,' said Dorothy. 'I pretended to be somebody else, naturally, but if people are being slow then sometimes one has to give them a little helping hand.'

'But why did you tell them that?'

'Because if one isn't in the papers then one might as well be dead. And everyone was talking about Augusta Laing getting the part, so I thought it was time I reminded them that she's nobody, and that I'm far more interesting than she is. And besides,' she added casually, 'I was doing you a favour. You're going to be the new boy in Hollywood, and you need to get off on the right foot.'

'But it will be in all the papers, won't it? I already have a girl, and she won't be too happy when she reads it.'

'Oh, you have a girl, do you? Well, she won't last long. I dare say I've done her a good turn, too. Better let her down gently now rather than string her along. She can't last, you know. And this is much more important. The publicity will do us both good. We're starring in this picture together, and people go wild for two romantic leads who are also in love off the screen.'

'But we're not.'

'Who cares?' she said. 'The public believe it, and that's all that matters.'

Robert Kenrick was dismayed.

'But I mean to say, Sarah really won't be happy, as she's rather the worrying kind. And her mother never approved of me much to start with, because I'm an actor, you know. What if they believe it too? I shall be in the most awful trouble. I think I shall have to call the papers to deny it. No offence meant, Dorothy, but I don't want them getting the wrong end of the stick.'

Dorothy Dacres pursed her lips in displeasure.

'Better not, darling,' she said. 'You're in it now, whether you like it or not. You'll soon see it's how things work in this business.'

'But—'

'Besides,' she went on, twisting a lock of her beautiful golden hair around her finger and gazing at him with innocent eyes, 'you don't want people to think you're not interested in me, do you? A lot of men would kill to be in your shoes right now. If people get even the tiniest idea that you're not keen on women then they might start to wonder.'

'Wonder what?'

'Oh, you know. You'd be surprised how rumours get around. People will talk, and Hollywood is very sensitive about the morality of its stars. I could tell you stories of people who've been black-listed for that kind of thing.'

'I don't know what you mean,' said Kenrick, taken aback.

'Don't you? Well, never mind. Let's just say that if you don't want to find yourself on the first boat home you'd be better off doing as I tell you. It's only for a little while. And you'll soon see there are a lot of beautiful girls in America. Far better looking than this Sally of yours, I'll bet.'

'Sarah.'

She waved a hand and promptly forgot the subject, leaving Robert Kenrick in a state of some perturbation as he absorbed his first unpleasant lesson in Hollywood politics. He said no more, but wandered back out onto the terrace—although this time the view did not appeal quite as much as it had before.

A young woman who bore some resemblance to Miss Dacres, albeit with darker hair and eyes, came into the living-room, bearing a huge bouquet of flowers.

'These just came from Mr. Aston,' she said.

'Oh, aren't they just divine?' said Dorothy, giving them the briefest of glances. 'Eugene, darling,' she said, calling to a man who was talking loudly and urgently on the telephone at the other side of the room. 'Is that Henry? Thank him for the flowers, won't you?'

The man addressed as Eugene nodded and carried on talking. Eventually he put the telephone down and came across.

'We're all set,' he said.

Dorothy was examining her fingernails idly.

'Do you know,' she said, 'one of those horrid press-men outside said that Augusta Laing is going to be Helen Harper. He must have been talking to Kenneth Neale. You know he doesn't want me to have the part. You don't think he's going to pull some stunt, do you?'

'Don't worry about him,' he replied. 'He's all talk, but he'll play ball. There's too much money at stake not to.'

Eugene S. Penk was the man Freddy had seen arriving with Seymour Cosgrove. Despite his rough and pugilistic appearance, he was in fact a rich and powerful man. He had started his career as a professional boxer, then had moved into the film business, first as an extra, then as a stunt-man and bit-part actor, until he had worked his way up to become head of production at one of the biggest Hollywood studios. But working for others did not suit him, and he had warred constantly with the studio executives. At last he had decided to strike out on his own, and had recently formed his own company, Aston-Penk Productions, in partnership with Henry Aston II, the son of the late industrial tycoon, who provided the financial backing. Their first two pictures had not been successes, and it had begun to look as though the venture were destined to fail, for Aston knew little about the film business and was a nervous investor, alternately trying to interfere and threatening to withdraw. However, Penk had made every effort to convince him that *For Every Yesterday* would be a hit, and hoped that the danger had passed for the moment.

'Now listen, Dorothy,' Penk went on. 'That's something I wanted to talk to you about. You've got to switch that famous charm of yours on and start talking nice to Kenneth Neale. I promised Henry I'd get him over to Hollywood, and I've got to do it. But I can't do it with you getting his wife all riled up every time you see her.'

'Why should I be nice to him when he doesn't want me in his picture?' said Dorothy, pouting a little.

'Because he's the best director in Europe and I want to hire him,' said Penk impatiently. 'And Henry wants him too. We've got to make a success of this one, or we're all going to be on the skids.'

'Oh, nonsense. One director is just like another. And who's heard of him back in the States? What's he done that anyone cares about? Nothing that I recall. *I'm* the one they're paying to see, and I think people ought to remember that a little more often when they tell me I can't have what I want.'

'Now, you're not going to start being difficult, are you?' said Penk. 'If he pulls out then we have to begin all over again, and Henry will get the heebie-jeebies, and you might find yourself without a part.'

'Well, all right, then,' said Dorothy with a sulky toss of her immaculate head. 'I'll play nice. Anyway, I didn't mean to upset Patience. But that ghastly child of theirs really is the limit. Do we have to have her in the movie?'

'Yes we do. She's a big hit over here with the British. They adore her, and she's the surest way of getting them to come and see it. And the surest way of getting Neale to come to Hollywood, too,' he added. 'We hire his little girl, we make him happy and he does whatever we want.'

'Ugh,' said Dorothy, wrinkling up her nose in disgust. 'So we have to have this Adorable Ada, or whatever she's called, and I guess Augusta Laing will be hanging around wanting a supporting rôle too, now that I've been given the plum one. I can't think why Kenneth wants Augusta so badly,' she went on petulantly. 'It's not even as though she's all that pretty. That hair of hers! It quite blinds one. And her acting is so insipid. Of course, with a little more experience she mightn't be *too* bad one day, but I don't think she's cut out for leading rôles—and she most certainly can't carry the part of Helen.'

'You have to admit she's closer to the right age,' said the young woman who had brought the flowers. 'It's a long time since you saw twenty-five.'

Dorothy sat up suddenly and glared at her.

'At least I can still *pass* for twenty-five,' she said. She looked the other woman up and down. 'Such a pity the camera never loved you as much as it did me, isn't it, darling? It always made you look so old and haggard. Why, no-one would ever have guessed that I'm seven years older than you. Do you know, Seymour,' she went on, addressing the photographer, 'there was more than one occasion when we were younger that Cora and I were mistaken for twins—by age, I mean. Not by resemblance.'

'Are you sure about that?' said Cora sweetly. 'As I recall, most people commented on how mature you looked for your age.

18

And most of your parts lately have been characters much older than you. What was that last one you did two years ago? I can't quite remember the name—but then I guess no-one else can either. It's such a shame how one can go from being the latest thing to nobody at all in just a few months. It can't be because of your age that you're not getting the parts any more, though, can it? I mean, after all, you just told me you can still pass for twenty-five.'

'Yes I can,' said Dorothy. 'And *that's* why I'm going to play Helen Harper.' She returned her sister's sweet smile. 'This is a hard business, and only the very best make it. I think you made a wise decision when you retired. Stars come and go, but Hollywood will always need secretaries and assistants like you.'

Cora flushed, but said nothing more, as Seymour Cosgrove, who had ignored—or perhaps not heard—the exchange, broke in and said:

'I think we're ready now. Dorothy, I want you over here by the piano.'

Dorothy swung herself up from the sofa with languorous grace and did as she was bid.

'Just lean against it like that,' said Seymour, and peered through the view-finder. A shade of doubt passed over his face.

'That dress—the colour's no good,' he said finally. 'It won't show up. You'll have to put a paler one on.'

'I have something in eau de nil,' said Dorothy. 'Mildred, bring it out—and the white silk too.'

A silent maid duly brought out several frocks and submitted them to the judgment of the photographer, who held them up one by one against Miss Dacres and squinted at her dispassionately. At last, he selected an evening-dress in pale blue.

'How does this one drape?' he said, then, without waiting for an answer: 'Go and put it on.'

At last she was dressed to his satisfaction, and the session began. Everybody watched as Dorothy Dacres struck a range of artistic and occasionally outlandish poses according to Cosgrove's instructions, while he took pictures from several different angles.

'Now you,' he said at last to Robert Kenrick. 'Come and stand next to her.'

'You're so dreadfully blunt and rude,' said Dorothy to Cosgrove. 'But I don't mind it. You always take such beautiful photos. Did Eugene tell you you're going to be working with me for the rest of this movie?'

'No can do,' said the photographer as he worked. 'Didn't I mention it? I'm off to America next week. *Out Of Town* have come across with the contract at last. I'm to be exclusive with them for five years. If there hadn't been a little delay I shouldn't even be here today. That's right—gaze into his eyes. Now turn to the camera and give a sidelong glance as though you knew something he didn't.'

'Silly,' said Dorothy. 'That's all off now.'

'What do you mean, it's all off now?'

'Why, I told them you wouldn't be coming,' she said, opening her eyes wide as though it were obvious.

'You told them *what*?' said Seymour Cosgrove. For the first time he looked up from his equipment and at Miss Dacres.

'I said you weren't coming. I need you here,' she explained. 'You don't mind, do you? There's no-one else can capture Dorothy Dacres like you do, and since this movie is to be my come-back, in a manner of speaking—not that I ever went away, of course—I'm going to need all the help I can get. This rôle is going to be a triumph for me, I can feel it, and I want you to be a part of it.'

'But I don't want to be a part of it,' said Cosgrove. He pulled at his hair, and seemed stunned. 'I want to go to the States and take pictures for magazines. *Out Of Town* are paying me a ridiculous amount of money to go over there, and they're going to let me do whatever I want. I'll have full artistic control. This is the opportunity I've been waiting for ever since I started in this business.'

'Oh, well, as to the money, I'm sure Eugene will match that,' said Dorothy. 'You will, won't you, Eugene?'

'What?' said Eugene Penk, to whom this was all evidently news.

'Well, that's settled, then,' said Dorothy. 'We'll pay you whatever you want. You can go to the States any time, but this is my big chance to show that I can do talkies just as well as regular pictures, so you see how important it is that you stay here and photograph me whenever I need you.'

Seymour looked as though he were building up to an explosion. He began to stride up and down.

'But I don't think you quite understand,' he said. 'I've been negotiating this for months now, and it was all settled at last. They're looking forward to my arrival—they said so. They have lots of things ready for me to do.'

'Don't worry, they didn't mind at all,' said Dorothy. 'Harry Adams is an old friend of mine, and he said they'll get Dickie Sanders across instead.'

'*What?*' said Seymour, coming to a sudden halt. His hair was standing on end from all the pulling. 'Dickie Sanders? *Dickie Sanders?* That—why—he couldn't—idiot—what—'

His rage had rendered him temporarily incoherent. Cora and Penk exchanged glances, while Dorothy looked wholly unconcerned, and even slightly surprised at his reaction. Her surprise was all the greater when Seymour strode up to her and gripped her by the arms.

'Hey, what do you think you're doing?' she said.

For a moment, Seymour seemed as though he were about to shake her, then he thought better of it and stepped back, breathing heavily.

'You—you—*stupid* woman!' he exclaimed, and with that, stormed out.

'Now you've gone and done it,' said Cora. 'Let's just hope he comes back.'

'Sure he'll come back,' said Dorothy, disconcerted. 'He'll have to, to get his things.'

'But what did you have to do that to him for?'

'Why, because I needed him. I never thought he would be so upset about it, though.'

'You don't say,' said her sister dryly.

'He'll be fine when he's calmed down,' said Dorothy. 'He does this all the time. We have fights but they don't mean anything.'

'Well, you'd better hope he's gotten over it by tomorrow,' said Penk. 'We need him here for the big party.'

'Oh, yes!' exclaimed Dorothy in sudden excitement, clapping her hands together. We are all set for tomorrow, aren't we, Eugene? I mean, you're going to announce that I've got the part?'

'I guess so,' said Penk. 'We can't keep it a secret forever, and half the world seems to know about it already.'

'Oh, good! I can't wait to see the look on Augusta's face when she hears. Maybe I'll go apologize to Seymour, and get him to take a photo of her just after she finds out. Wouldn't I just love to see that picture!'

'You can try,' said Cora. 'But I doubt you'll get far. Didn't you know he's sweet on her?'

'Really?' said Dorothy in surprise. 'I can't think why.'

She immediately forgot about Seymour and her unfortunate rival Augusta Laing, and struck a dramatic pose that any of her fans would have recognized from the publicity posters for her last film.

'I can't wait for tomorrow,' she said. 'This is going to be such a triumph for me!'

CHAPTER THREE

IN A TERRACED house in an unfashionable part of London which one might as well call Highbury, the film director Kenneth Neale was talking to Augusta Laing on the telephone.

'I think you're sure of the part,' he was saying. 'Penk told me so in confidence, but I expect we'll find out for certain at this party tonight.'

He paused to listen.

'Well, one never knows with Americans,' he said. 'But I should say you were a dead cert. If they've got an ounce of sense they'll see that the Dacres woman is all wrong for Helen. She's got the wrong face—and that voice of hers! No, don't give it another thought. Put on your best frock, and we'll show them all that we British can put on every bit as good a display as they can.'

He put down the receiver and turned to his wife. Kenneth Neale was short and wide, with a face which was nondescript when at rest, but extraordinarily expressive when he chose to make it so. He was the son of a well-off fishmonger, and, through hard work and great natural talent, had ascended from these relatively humble beginnings to become one of the most respected film directors in Europe. Not for him the privileges of public school and the best universities; no, everything he had attained—and this was not inconsiderable—had been through his own efforts entirely, for in the breast of this son of a tradesman there burned the soul of an artist. He had seen his first moving picture as a child around the turn of the century, and had been instantly enraptured by it. From then on he had rejected all attempts to interest him in the business of wholesale fish trading—even though there was a good living and a family concern waiting for him should he have chosen to take it up—but had left all that to his younger brother, devoting himself instead to this brave new world. Now he was fêted all over Europe for his artistry, and Hollywood was beckoning. He was indifferent to look at, his accent was not the thing at all, and he required constant reminding about his table manners when dining in public—and yet he must have had something about him, for he had managed first to woo and then to marry a Cabinet Secretary's daughter, who had had two successful seasons in London and might have picked and chosen from the best of the country's young men. Uncharitable types might have whispered that her looks tended towards the equine and her teeth were unfortunate, but the Neales were quite oblivious to what other people thought, and had fallen in love and married without its occurring to them to ask for anybody else's approval.

'Must we go to this party?' said Patience Neale, who was sitting at the breakfast-table, drinking tea. She exuded exquisite good breeding. 'It's such a bore, having to talk to all these people who have nothing to say unless it's about themselves and how marvellous they are.'

'I'm afraid we must, my sweet,' said Kenneth Neale. 'Penk is going to announce me as director of *For Every Yesterday*, and Augusta as Helen Harper, and it wouldn't do to miss it. I expect he also wants to have another shot at talking me into coming to Hollywood.'

'But I thought you said you had more artistic freedom here in England,' said Patience.

'I thought so—perhaps I still do,' said Neale. 'But he had a lot to say about the new recording techniques. I admit I used to have my doubts about whether they could work reliably, but that last one we did went down very well—far better than I'd expected, as a matter of fact. They're doing some marvellous things with sound these days, and the big studios are all investing heavily in it. The Americans are a little bit ahead of us there, and we shouldn't need to stay more than a year or two if you didn't like it. Besides, they're promising great things for Ada, and she's at that tricky age. A few years more and she'll be too old for child parts. This is her big chance to conquer America and become a real star, just as she deserves.'

'Should you like to go to Hollywood, darling?' said Patience.

This last question was addressed to a child of seven who was sitting next to her mother at the table—a little girl of such exquisite beauty that one could have been forgiven for thinking it impossible that she could be in any way related to Mr. and Mrs. Neale. And yet, by some odd quirk of biology, they had produced this doll of a child, Ada—a spoilt, petted, beloved darling, who was already well known to the British public as Adorable Ada. Her innocent smile and sweet singing voice had won her national fame, and she had already appeared in three comic films and made several gramophone records. Thanks to her early success, this young person was possessed of an almost preternatural degree of assurance and composure. She now put her head on one side and considered.

'I expect it will be an *in*-teresting experience,' she pronounced at last.

'Well, we'll see,' said Patience Neale. 'I don't know that I like the idea. America always sounds so uncivilized to me. Still, you must be sure and do the best you can in this film, Ada. This is to be a serious part—not like your usual ones—and you shall have to talk, too.'

'I imagine it will be easy enough,' said Ada. 'I can do most things, you know.'

And with that little exhibition of self-confidence she went back to eating her buttered toast.

'Why is this party at Dorothy Dacres' hotel, if Augusta is to play Helen?' said Patience to her husband. 'Dorothy's been in London a few weeks now, and you know she's been angling for the part. You don't suppose you've got it all wrong, do you, dear?'

'Not a chance,' said Neale. 'I told Penk in no uncertain terms that she's no good, and he agreed with me privately, and said he couldn't stop her from coming here and acting as though it's in the bag, but he'd see to it that she didn't get it. There's a question of squaring things with his backers, though. Dacres is over here because Henry Aston has told her he wants her for the part, and she thinks he has the last word. But Penk says he's pretty sure he can convince Aston that Augusta will be much better. And she will be, too. Who'd want to see an American play Helen Harper? Why, her character is English through and through, and this is a talkie, so everyone will hear straightaway that her voice is all wrong.'

'And she's so rude, too,' murmured Patience. 'She was quite horrid to poor Ada. You were dreadfully upset, weren't you darling?'

'Perhaps a little,' said Ada. 'She wasn't especially nice, but I expect she was jealous. Older women are always envious when younger girls come along and make them look ugly. I know I'm not a woman yet, but I don't have any wrinkles like she does, and I imagine it reminds her of how old she is.'

'Does she have wrinkles?' said Patience. 'I can't say I'd noticed.'

'Oh, yes. All women over twenty have wrinkles,' said Ada, with an air of authority. 'And their ankles get fat, too. I should hate to be twenty. I shall retire at nineteen and go and live by the sea.'

'Goodness,' said Patience, glancing involuntarily at her own ankles, of which she had always been rather proud. 'Anyway,' she went on to her husband. 'Augusta is simply nicer, too, and since you're the one who will have to work with them all, I suggest you see to it that Dorothy doesn't get her own way and play Helen Harper.'

'Oh, don't you worry about that,' said Neale. 'I'll see to it all right.'

CHAPTER FOUR

ON WEDNESDAY EVENING Freddy and two friends of his betook themselves to a new restaurant near Brook Street that was meant to be quite the latest thing. The dinner was something of a disappointment, but the crowd was a fashionable one, and afforded plenty of opportunity to observe the goings-on of certain people who ought to have known better—a good thing, too, for it turned out that Freddy's friends had decided that very day to get engaged to one another, and he was finding himself uncomfortably *de trop*, and glad of any excuse to look away from them. Eventually he spotted someone he knew, and excused himself, leaving the love-birds to bill and coo as much as they liked. He spent some time in conversation, then made up his mind to return to his table and tell his friends he was going home. Threading his way among the closely-packed tables he bumped into a young woman with flaming red hair going the other way, who started and peered more closely at him.

'Why, if it isn't Freddy Pilkington-Soames!' she exclaimed, then, as he looked uncertain, 'It's Gussie, you ass.'

'Gussie Lippincott!' he said in sudden recognition. 'Good Lord! Why, I haven't seen you since—when was it?'

'Haven't the foggiest,' she said cheerfully. 'But I expect it's been aeons. You're looking well, I must say.'

'Not as well as you,' he said. 'You're positively blooming. How's the Bishop?'

'Oh, Pops is getting pretty doddery now—although he'll deny it. The poor dear could never cope with three daughters even in his younger days. But Pam looks after him nicely, and doesn't mind a bit. I've run away to London, as you can see.'

Gussie Lippincott was the youngest daughter of the Bishop of Pilborough. As a child she had been plain and awkward, and had wanted nothing more than for her bright orange hair to turn golden like that of her two sisters. Now, at twenty-two, her beauty was nothing less than breathtaking, for the red hair had become a gleaming copper halo, below which a pair of green eyes glinted wickedly, promising only mischief. Her smile was dazzling, and she bestowed it generously on all-comers, for she had always been a good-natured sort, and it seemed as though she had not changed in that respect. She and Freddy now beamed at one another as two old friends who have not met for some years, until called to attention by an irritated cough from the man by whose chair they were standing, preventing him from easily reaching his glass of wine.

'Bother,' said Gussie as they moved hurriedly out of the way. 'This place is the limit. Where can we go and talk? I suppose you want to get back to your friends?'

'Not at all,' said Freddy, and explained.

'Oh, splendid. My lot are being a dreadful bore, and they won't miss me at all either. Listen, I'm supposed to be going to a party later. I was meant to be going with someone, but we've had a little disagreement. You wouldn't mind standing in, would you?'

Freddy was only too happy, and shortly afterwards the two of them emerged into the London night. The weather had continued dry, but there was still a sharp nip in the air, and Gussie Lippincott huddled into her thick fur coat and grasped Freddy's arm tightly as they walked through the streets of Mayfair.

'You must tell me what you've been doing with yourself,' she said. 'I heard you'd gone into the reporting business.'

'I have,' said Freddy. 'I work for the *Clarion*.'

'Is that so?' she said, eyeing him speculatively. 'That's rather handy.'

'Why?'

'Because I like seeing my name in the papers,' she said. 'I'm an actress now, you see.'

'Really? I hadn't heard about that. I don't recall reading your name anywhere.'

'You wouldn't. Of course I don't call myself Gussie Lippincott. Professionally I'm known as Augusta Laing.'

'Good Lord!' said Freddy again, coming to a sudden halt. 'Augusta Laing! Why, of course I've heard of you. I saw you in that film—what was it? The one with the train and the dead man. Was that really you? I should never have recognized you. I say, you're very good, aren't you?'

'Thank you,' she said modestly. 'One does one's best. And it really is the most enormous fun.'

'I expect it is. Oh—but aren't you supposed to be in this new picture that everybody's talking about?'

She grimaced.

'That's a sticky question,' she said. 'I've been dying to play Helen Harper. It's a part any serious actress would kill for, and I know Kenneth Neale wants me to do it—he's going to direct it, you know—but there's an American actress who wants the part, too.'

'Dorothy Dacres?' said Freddy.

'Oh, you've heard all about it, then?'

'In passing.'

'Well, I think she'd make an awful fist of it, and so does Ken, but there's no denying she's a huge star, whereas I'm pretty much a nobody at present. Helen would be my first really big leading rôle, and it would give my career the most tremendous leg-up—if I did it well, I mean—but I don't think I dare hope for it, even though Ken keeps telling me the part's mine.'

'You really want it, don't you?' said Freddy, looking at her.

'More than anything,' she said fiercely. Then her face relaxed into its usual smile. 'But don't listen to me maundering. Come along to this do with me. I have the feeling there's going to be a bit of excitement one way or another for you to put in your newspaper.'

'Oh, why's that?'

'Because Dorothy Dacres is throwing it. A lot of the people from the film are going to be there, including Eugene Penk, the producer, and I suspect they're going to make some announcement about it.'

'You mean that you've got the rôle?'

'I hope so, so terribly much. But I daren't bank on it,' she said. 'I'm rather worried Dorothy has something up her sleeve. I can't think why she's doing this otherwise.'

They now arrived at the Abingdon, and were ushered in and up to the sixth floor. Inside Dorothy Dacres' suite they found the party already in full swing, with crowds of people standing in groups, laughing and talking, while waiters darted about, serving drinks on trays. A man sat at the piano, playing a tune that Freddy recognized as one of the latest 'hits', while a woman stood next to him and sang.

'Why, isn't that the Kibbles?' he said.

'Basil and Birdie, yes,' said Gussie. 'I know Birdie is supposed to be playing the part of the maid in *For Every Yesterday*, so I expect that's why they're here. And that's Bob Kenrick over there. He's a terribly nice chap, and quite innocent—although I don't know how long that will last once Hollywood gets its hooks into him.'

Robert Kenrick was standing by the terrace door with a young woman who looked awkward and out of place. He seemed to be pointing out various well-known people to her, and she smiled wanly. As Freddy watched, Dorothy Dacres swept across, resplendent in a creation of pale pink chiffon and silver beading that must have cost fifty guineas at least. She looked Robert Kenrick's companion up and down with an air of chilly politeness and murmured something. The girl half-looked as though she were wondering whether to curtsey, but Dorothy turned away from her immediately and proceeded to direct the full force of her personality at Robert Kenrick. She brushed a speck of something from his jacket and smiled at him coyly from under her eyelashes. Then she pointed at someone across the room and led him away before he could say anything. Kenrick glanced back apologetically at his companion, who gazed at the floor for a minute and then went to sit on a chair by the wall, where she fidgeted with her bracelet and occasionally put a hand to her eye as though to stop a tear.

Freddy helped Gussie to a drink and took one for himself, then spotted a man with a large moustache standing at the other side of the room in among a group of people.

'I say,' he said suddenly. 'It's Sir Aldridge Featherstone.'

'Who?'

'He owns the *Clarion*. I wonder why he's here. Perhaps it's to do with business. I've heard he's been thinking of getting into films.'

'Chap with the bristles?' said Gussie in sudden interest. 'He owns the *Clarion*, you say? That's Kenneth and Patience Neale he's talking to. They're terribly nice people and have been very good to me. I'm rather a protégée of Ken's, you know. Come and say hallo.'

Introductions were made. Sir Aldridge eyed Gussie appreciatively, and Freddy with distant recognition.

'Ah, Pilkington-Soames, isn't it?' he said. 'I didn't know you chaps were coming. Bickerstaffe send you?'

'No, sir. I'm here with Miss Laing in a purely private capacity.'

'Splendid, splendid,' said Sir Aldridge, and looked admiringly at Gussie again. Gussie recognized an opportunity to court the press, and proceeded to enter into conversation with Sir Aldridge, with a view to charming him into printing favourable pieces about her. The Neales were talking to Lady Featherstone, and Freddy was about to join in with some remark when he heard a voice at his elbow.

'Hallo,' the voice said.

He turned and saw a child standing next to him. She was dressed in a white, frilled dress with a yellow sash which had been washed and pressed to perfection, and had not a spot on it. Her dark, curly hair was brushed and shiny, and a yellow bow was perched centrally on top of it, in seeming defiance of all the laws of childhood. Most children of Freddy's acquaintance tended to be covered in mud and other unmentionable substances, and as a rule had twigs in their hair, bleeding knees and socks around their ankles. This one looked as though it had been brought out of a box for the occasion.

'What's your name?' she said.

'I'm Freddy,' said Freddy.

'It's a pleasure to meet you. Are you in films?'

'No, I'm a newspaper reporter.'

'I'm in films,' said the child complacently. 'I expect you've heard of me. I'm Ada Neale, but I'm more commonly known as Adorable Ada.'

'Are you, indeed? Adorable, eh? But I'll bet you get up to enough mischief when nobody's looking, don't you?'

'No,' said Ada, regarding him pityingly. 'I'm adorable.' And to his astonishment she jumped and gave a twirl, then came to rest with her head on one side and hands under her chin, gazing up at him with a pretty smile that was full of bright-eyed humour.

'Of course,' he said.

In an instant the smile disappeared and she resumed her solemn demeanour as though nothing had happened.

'They say I'm very talented,' she said.

'I should say you are.'

She gazed around.

'Everyone is here for Dorothy Dacres,' she said. 'Do you like her?'

'Why, I couldn't say. I've never met her.'

'I don't like her. She's horrid and spiteful. She called me a brat.'

'I can't think why,' said Freddy.

'Mummy hates her too,' said Ada. 'Mummy hates anyone who is unkind to me.'

'And quite right, too.'

'I love Mummy,' she said, fixing him with a stare that seemed to defy him to contradict her. 'And I love Daddy too. He doesn't like Dorothy either. He'll be very cross if she gets the part of Helen Harper.'

'Come and speak to Mr. Penk, darling,' said Mrs. Neale. 'He wants to talk to you about the film.'

And with that the Neales went off. Sir Aldridge and Lady Featherstone had fallen into conversation with someone else, and Gussie and Freddy were left alone.

'I see you've met Ada,' she said.

'Is she a real child, or a mechanical doll?' said Freddy. 'She doesn't seem altogether human, somehow.'

'No, she doesn't, does she?' agreed Gussie. She was about to say something else when a young man suddenly presented himself before them.

'Hallo, Gussie,' he said, fixing her with a look of great concentration.

Gussie immediately became very cool and stiff.

'Hallo, Seymour,' she said distantly.

'You decided to come after all, then.'

'So you see.'

He turned to Freddy and held out a hand.

'Seymour Cosgrove,' was what he said, although to judge from the way his eyebrows were at that moment attempting to crawl down his nose, it was quite obvious that what he *wanted* to say was, 'And who the devil are you?'

'Freddy Pilkington-Soames,' said Freddy, and shook the hand.

'Freddy is a *very* old friend of mine,' said Gussie sweetly. 'We've known one another for years, haven't we, Freddy? Why, we practically grew up together.'

'I see,' said Seymour.

There was an uncomfortable silence as he and Gussie attempted to stare one another down.

'Hadn't you better go and mingle?' she said at last.

'All right, then,' he said, and without another word turned away and stalked off, defeated.

Gussie took Freddy's arm proprietorially.

'Come and meet people,' she said, and began chattering non-stop. Freddy noticed that her manner had suddenly become more flirtatious, and connected this, correctly, with the encounter with Seymour Cosgrove, for she kept glancing over at the part of the room to which Seymour had retired, as though to make sure he was watching.

'What was that little pantomime between you and Cosgrove?' he said.

'I have no idea what you mean,' said Gussie.

'Rot. He's the chap you've fallen out with, is that it? He's obviously in love with you. Why don't you go and make it up with him?'

'Because he's an idiot,' said Gussie with finality. 'Now, go and get me another drink and don't let's talk about him any more.'

Freddy went off to do as he was bid. After a brief search he spied a tall waiter carrying a tray of drinks, and made a bee-line for him, but the waiter just then seemed to remember something, and turned hurriedly away, so Freddy was forced to go and look for another one. The room was very hot, and the noise was getting louder. Birdie Kibble was now sitting on the piano, telling risqué jokes. She and her husband had been popular music-hall stars ten or fifteen years ago, and had made a successful transition to the screen, starring in a number of short comic films. The crowd gathered around the Kibbles laughed uproariously as Birdie lay back and played a short tune on the piano with her arms above her head.

Freddy finally managed to find a drink, and returned to discover that Gussie had already managed to procure one herself, and had entered into close conversation with another young woman. There was much giggling and glancing around, and Freddy sensed that he was no longer wanted. Taking advantage of the lull, he went out onto the terrace, which was a big one, and extended in a wide curve around the corner of the building. He wandered over to the edge. It was protected by a wall at about waist height, on top of which was a low railing. The night was clear and he could see stars. He lit a cigarette and was thinking about nothing in particular, when he slowly became aware of the sound of voices raised as though in an altercation. They were coming from around the corner, from a part of the terrace he could not see. A man said something, then a higher, female voice replied. Almost without thinking, Freddy drifted that way in case there was trouble, and was just in time to hear the woman say in an American accent:

'Well, just you remember you were nobody yesterday, and you could just as easily be nobody again tomorrow. I could make a couple of phone-calls right now and see to it that no-one in Hollywood will ever hire you—your name will be mud. Now, what do you think of that?'

The man said something inaudible, and Freddy moved away hurriedly as he came into view. It was Robert Kenrick, who was looking almost angry—an expression which did not suit him. He threw Freddy a glance and went back indoors. Dorothy Dacres appeared shortly afterwards, a complacent expression on her pretty face.

'Get me a drink, would you, darling?' she said to Freddy, then swept indoors and over to the crowd by the piano. She grabbed an empty glass and a cocktail spoon, and rang for silence.

'Well, isn't this nice?' she said, looking around her with an appearance of genuine pleasure. 'Thank you all so much for coming to my little celebration. You don't know how much it means to me to have received such a welcome here in London. Everybody has been so kind, and so I just know you'll be as pleased to hear what I have to announce as I am to announce it. Where's Eugene?'

Eugene Penk was located and summoned to the piano, and Dorothy touched his arm and went on:

'I wanted to keep the news a secret just a *little* while longer, but I've been bursting to tell, and Eugene says I may. Now, you know everybody's been talking about the film production of *For Every Yesterday*, and the part of Helen Harper. It's such a classic piece of English theatre that I wasn't at all sure I was right for the rôle, being a silly old American and all, but—well, I let myself be persuaded into an audition, and I'm so happy to tell you that yesterday I finally got the news that I'm to play the part! Now, isn't that just grand?'

Here she paused and beamed round, as everybody burst into applause. Freddy looked around and saw Gussie Lippincott standing and staring across at Dorothy Dacres. It was impossible to read her expression, or to see what she was feeling.

'Someone's going to murder that woman one day,' murmured a voice at his shoulder just then, and he turned to see Seymour Cosgrove standing next to him. It seemed as though he had been talking to himself, for he looked up and saw Freddy, then shrugged and moved away.

Dorothy was still talking, demanding everyone's congratulations, gushing that she hoped she could do justice to the rôle of

Helen, when it had always been meant for an Englishwoman. Freddy glanced around again, but Gussie had disappeared. He hoped she was not too disappointed, although he feared it must have been a blow to her. Perhaps he would take her another drink and commiserate with her. He was not sure of the correct thing to say in such circumstances, but at least he could try. He glanced around for a waiter, but there was none nearby. Everybody was still watching Dorothy Dacres. At that moment, Freddy spotted the tall waiter he had seen earlier, standing by a door, looking about him surreptitiously, and his jaw dropped. The waiter had not seen Freddy, and slipped quietly into the next room. Freddy followed him.

On the other side of the door was a bedroom. It was surely not palatial enough to be that of Dorothy Dacres, but it was certainly luxurious, for a large bed dressed with silk cushions stood in the centre of the room, while the curtains were of thick velvet, and the dressing-table and other furnishings were of expensive-looking polished walnut. The man was busy searching through the dressing-table, and did not hear Freddy come in. At last he shut a drawer with a sigh, then glanced up and into the mirror, whereupon he caught sight of Freddy's reflection behind him. The start he gave was almost comical, and he whirled around.

'What the devil do you think you're doing, Corky?' said Freddy.

CHAPTER FIVE

CORKY BECKWITH LOOKED as though he were about to deny everything, but since he had been caught redhanded in the very act of rifling through a drawer in a private hotel-room, he thought better of it and decided to brazen it out.

'Freddy, old chap!' he exclaimed. 'How simply spiffing to see you. Delightful party, what?'

'Why are you dressed as a waiter?' said Freddy.

Corky looked down at himself in affected surprise.

'Oh, this,' he said. 'It's a very long and tragic story, and all starts with the death of a great-aunt of mine. We'd rather been relying on the will, but it turned out she'd hidden all her money in the hollow of her wooden leg, and didn't think to tell anybody before she died. It wasn't until she'd already been cremated that we found the letter under her pillow explaining where she'd put it. So, being as I am somewhat embarrassed for funds at the moment, I have been forced to take a job on the side, as it were, in order to make ends meet.'

'Rot,' said Freddy. 'You're up to something. Did the *Herald* send you, or are you free-lancing? Do they know you're breaking into people's rooms?'

'I haven't broken into anywhere. If people *will* leave doors unlocked then they must expect others to enter.'

'But what are you looking for?'

'I couldn't possibly tell you,' said Corky. 'Go and find your own story. Goodness knows, I've had to tell enough lies to get this job, and I've been getting up at half past five in the morning for three weeks now—' here he shuddered, '—so if you think I'm going to give all that hard work away and let you barge in and steal the glory you've got another think coming.' He regarded Freddy's dinner-suit with some disfavour. 'I see you managed to stroll in here with an invitation. Go and talk to your society pals and see what they'll tell you. But I expect you already know all about it and are keeping quiet.'

'Keeping quiet about what?'

Corky pursed his lips and wagged his finger infuriatingly.

'You'd better spill the beans,' said Freddy, 'unless you want me to blow your disguise. I don't know how the Abingdon will take it if they find out one of their employees has been gaily burgling the patrons, but I imagine the police will come into it somewhere.'

'You wouldn't!' said Corky, aghast. 'Why, squeal on a man who's just trying to earn an honest living? What sort of a rotter are you?'

'The sort who gets his stories on the up-and-up, without rummaging through people's underthings,' said Freddy shamelessly. 'Now, tell me what you've got, or else.'

Corky looked sulky.

'It's nothing much,' he said. 'Only we've had a rumour that snow is falling in high places, if you catch my meaning. These film people fling the stuff about all over the shop, as I'm sure you're very aware. As a matter of fact, I shouldn't be a bit surprised to discover you were up to the eyes in it yourself. You have that red-rimmed look about you at times, and some of your copy is quite frankly incomprehensible, especially on a Monday.'

He gave an insinuating leer that showed all his teeth, and looked Freddy up and down.

'I see,' said Freddy. 'You want to catch someone in the act, have them arrested and get a nice little moralizing piece out of it.'

'That's about the size of it,' agreed Corky. 'But not only that, of course. Someone has to supply these incurable degenerates with the white powder, and I mean to find out who it is. I'm friendly with some of the chaps at Scotland Yard, and they've been giving me the low-down. If I can catch whoever's been slipping the goods to these acting people, it will be the most tremendous scoop for me.' He paused to reflect pleasurably on the praise that would be showered upon him if his scheme came off. 'I say,' he went on, 'I don't suppose you know anything you'd be prepared to tell, do you, old chap?'

'Not a thing,' said Freddy truthfully. 'I barely know anyone here. Augusta Laing is an old friend of mine and I've come with her.'

'Augusta Laing, eh?' said Corky, with another leer. 'Juicy little piece, isn't she?'

'I'm so glad you've decided not to bother with any of that class and refinement nonsense,' said Freddy. 'I expect the *Herald* has already pencilled you in to cover next year's debutantes' ball, yes?'

'Oh, it has, it has. Did I tell you they've given me a rise? They seemed to think I'd done rather well on that little story about the Lord Chamberlain. Such a pity the *Clarion* never got so much as a whiff of it, don't you think? But then, you were all probably too busy sucking up to Mrs. Belcher to notice what was going on.'

Freddy ignored this jibe, for it was perfectly true that the *Clarion* had done badly on the scandal.

'This is all beside the point,' he said. 'You've been rumbled now so you'd better get out. You'll have to find some other way to get your story.'

Corky looked mutinous.

'But I haven't finished looking,' he said. 'There's the maid's room to search yet.'

'Do you really suppose the maid takes cocaine?' said Freddy. 'Stop being an ass and get out before I report you to somebody.'

'But I can't go yet,' said Corky. 'I can't leave them short-handed. Strange as it may seem to you, I do take a certain pride in my work. My fellow-waiters have been so kind as to say it's almost as though I'd been born to the business, and I don't want to let them down. There are a hundred people out there, all wanting champagne. If I go now then Jenkins will have to do an extra shift, although he's desperate to get home to his sick wife.'

He spoke with sincerity, and Freddy relented.

'All right, then,' he said. 'Stay if you must—but just for this evening. After that, you'd better scoot, and I warn you, I shall be keeping an eye on you.'

'You know me as a man of my word,' said Corky gratefully, and slipped out of the room.

'Only if the word is "fathead,"' said Freddy under his breath. He waited a moment, thinking it might draw unwelcome attention if they both left at once, and as he did so, he noticed through a gap in the curtains that in this bedroom was another door giving onto the main terrace. He went across and peered out. This corner of the terrace was quite secluded, and out of sight of the entertaining area that led from the living-room. It was deserted. He felt a cold draught and realized that the door was ajar, and so pulled it shut, but did not lock it in case anyone wanted to come in that way. When he emerged into the living-room, he found that Gussie was still nowhere to be seen. The music had stopped, for Basil and Birdie had deserted their positions by the piano. Birdie was talking to Sir Aldridge; from across the room Freddy could hear the sound of her raucous laugh as she told some amusing anecdote.

'I don't suppose you've seen Augusta Laing, have you?' he said to a young woman sitting in a chair by the wall. She was the girl who had arrived with Robert Kenrick, and she looked thoroughly fed up. She shook her head. Kenrick also seemed to have disappeared, and Freddy wondered whether the girl intended to stay in the same chair all evening. Under ordinary circumstances he would have taken pity on her and engaged her in conversation, but he was worried about Gussie and wanted to find her. He roved around the room, but could not see her. Corky Beckwith was hovering near another door with a tray of drinks, and Freddy eyed him suspiciously. Corky saw he had been spotted and looked momentarily cross, but then gave Freddy an ingratiating smile and moved away to another part of the room. Freddy eyed the door, wondering what was behind it, just as Eugene Penk passed him and went through it, followed by Kenneth Neale. Perhaps Gussie had gone that way too. Freddy went over and just glanced through the door into the room beyond. This, he judged, was Dorothy Dacres' bedroom, for it was several degrees more luxurious than the other one. The room was empty, but a double glass door on the other side of it led out onto what was presumably a second terrace. The door was standing slightly open, and it looked as though Penk and Neale had gone that way. Freddy had no wish to interrupt, and so returned to the living-room and entered into conversation with Lady Featherstone. She then drifted away, and he was left to make fatuous conversation with a group of young men who appeared to have come for the free drinks.

Suddenly Gussie was standing before him. She was bright-eyed and wearing a brittle smile.

'There you are,' she said. 'I've been searching for you everywhere. I want you to tell me what a wonderful actress I am and make me feel better.'

'You are a wonderful actress,' he replied. 'All the critics say so, and I've seen it myself.'

'Never mind that. You don't know the half of it. I've put on the performance of my life this evening. I've been simply seething with disappointment since they made the announcement, but I've smiled and congratulated Dorothy, and talked about how marvellous it will be to have her here in England for a month or two, and I've simpered prettily when people have congratulated me on getting the supporting rôle—oh, yes, to add insult to injury they're going to make me work with the woman and watch her ruin the part that ought to have been mine—and I've agreed that it won't matter if her accent isn't right, and altogether I've chirped and chattered as gaily as if I'd got the part myself.'

'Well done,' said Freddy in sympathy.

'I shall keep it up to the bitter end, too,' she went on, 'and no-one shall ever know that I'm feeling sick to my stomach about the whole affair.'

'I'm sorry, old girl,' he said.

'I hate her, of course,' she said conversationally. 'In fact, I rather wish she were dead, but it doesn't do to say that sort of thing in public.'

'You can say it to me. I won't tell a soul. And I quite understand.'

She smiled.

'Thank you, Freddy. It's kind of you to listen to me. I'll get over the disappointment—after all, it's hardly the end of the world. But Ken will be dreadfully upset too, I'm afraid. Where is he? I haven't had the chance to speak to him about it.'

At that moment they saw Kenneth Neale come out of Dorothy's room with a face like thunder.

'Oh dear,' said Gussie. 'I shall leave him to Patience's kindly ministrations. I expect he'll need some time to calm down.

Come out on the terrace. I'm feeling a little hot and bothered after all this.'

They went outside. The terrace was deserted apart from two people who were standing together in conversation by the railing. One of them was Robert Kenrick, who saw them and turned away to look out over the rooftops. The other was the girl Freddy had seen talking to Gussie earlier, who glanced back at Kenrick and hurried over to them.

'Oh, Augusta, I'm so sorry!' she said, and burst into tears.

'Why, whatever's the matter, Cora?' said Gussie.

Cora threw up her hands.

'All this, of course,' she said. 'I knew, you see. I knew Dorothy was going to get the part and I ought to have warned you, but they wouldn't let me tell. I'm so very sorry. I wish I'd never come to England. It's been nothing but trouble from the start.'

'Don't give it a second thought, darling,' said Gussie. 'I suppose it was a foregone conclusion really. I couldn't hope to have got the part once Dorothy came on the scene. It wasn't your fault.'

'She causes trouble wherever she goes,' said Cora. 'She lost Seymour his job, you know. He was all set to go to the States and take pictures for that magazine, but she wanted him here so she called them and told them he wasn't coming. I'm surprised he's here this evening. And she's upset Bob, too.' She indicated Robert Kenrick, who was leaning over the railing and smoking with great determination. After a moment he realized they were all looking at him and scowled, then turned away and went back inside. Cora sobbed again and shivered.

The noise from inside seemed to be getting louder. They heard a shriek of laughter from somewhere nearby.

'We'd better go back in,' said Cora. 'How noisy London is, even in the middle of the week. Doesn't anybody ever sleep in this city?'

'I suppose I'll go and speak to Dorothy again,' said Gussie, as they went inside and Cora shut the door. 'I didn't get the chance to speak to her for long, and I don't want her to think I'm upset. Where is she, by the way? I haven't seen her for ages.'

'I don't know. She was by the piano,' said Cora. 'I'll go see if I can find her.'

She hurried off, and Gussie went to talk to Patience Neale. Basil and Birdie Kibble had returned to the piano and the music had started again, although more quietly this time. Freddy drifted across to where they were sitting. From a distance they seemed a youthful pair, but close up he now saw that they were both wearing thick stage make-up, and were obviously much older than they appeared.

'Hallo, hallo,' said Basil Kibble. 'A little bird tells me you're press.'

Freddy saw that the paint had collected in the creases at the corners of his eyes, and that his hair was a suspiciously rich shade of dark brown.

'That's true,' he said.

'I thought this was meant to be a private party,' said Basil.

'So it is. I came with Gussie—Augusta, I mean. Rather a jolly do, what?'

'Oh, we're having a fine time!' said Birdie, and laughed uproariously. 'We always do, don't we, Basil?'

'Splendid,' said Freddy. 'I'm pleased to hear it. I understand you're going to be in this film,' he went on, addressing Birdie.

'Oh, yes, oh yes indeed!' she exclaimed. Her eyes fairly gleamed with excitement at the prospect. 'It'll be nice to get back in front of the camera, although nothing beats the stage. You don't hear the applause in a studio,' she explained. 'Music to our ears, that sound is.'

'It certainly is,' agreed Basil, and rattled off a few chords. The two of them seemed far more cheerful than anyone else at the party—but then all this business about the rôle of Helen Harper did not affect them in the slightest.

'Hallo, Birdie,' said Gussie, joining them just then. 'Have you seen Dorothy?'

'Can't say I have,' said Birdie. 'Where's she disappeared to, then?'

Just then a bell rang, and Freddy saw the door to the suite open and admit a man. From the looks of him he was some high functionary at the hotel. He appeared to be casting his eyes about for a person in authority. At last he spotted Eugene Penk, who had just come out of Dorothy's room and loudly demanded a drink, and approached him discreetly, a serious expression on his face. From the other side of the room a commotion was happening. There was a bustle of excitement and some shrieking. Something seemed to be going on outside, for there was a little rush towards the terrace. Seymour Cosgrove came across to Penk, his face twisted into an expression of distaste. Penk glanced at the functionary and held up his hand to arrest him before he could begin to speak.

'What's all that noise?' he said to Seymour. 'Why's every-body going outside all of a sudden?'

'They're saying there's been an accident in the street,' said Seymour. 'Someone's been run over or something, and they've all gone out to have a look. Rather ghoulish, if you ask me.'

The functionary was coughing and doing his best to attract Penk's attention.

'Yes, what is it?' said Penk impatiently.

The functionary said something in a low voice.

'*What?*' exclaimed Penk and Seymour at the same time.

There was more urgent conferring. Freddy was now watch-ing with the greatest interest. Seymour looked aghast, and Penk set his jaw. At that moment there was a scream.

'It's Dorothy!' shouted someone. The cry was quickly taken up, and more people rushed for the terrace. The functionary now spoke again, and this time Freddy could hear his voice clearly.

'Yes, sir. It appears Miss Dacres fell from the terrace. I'm ter-ribly afraid she's dead.'

CHAPTER SIX

ON RECEIVING THE news, Eugene Penk stood rooted to the spot, but only for a moment. Then he swiftly took charge.

'Get all these people off the terrace,' he said. He strode across the room, followed by Seymour, and started ordering, shooing and cajoling people back inside, with the strength of personality that had seen him rise to the powerful position he held today. Once everybody was inside, he stood in front of the door, with an expression designed to repel all comers.

'You,' he said, beckoning to a nearby waiter. 'Keep everybody back.'

The functionary nodded to the waiter in agreement, and then he and Penk went out onto the terrace. Freddy, who had been watching the scene closely, now melted away from the crowd gathered around the door, and slipped quietly back into the room in which he had found Corky earlier. It was empty. He dimmed the light, then went across to the second set of terrace doors and pulled them open a little way, standing behind the curtain so as not to be seen from the outside. After a moment, Penk and the functionary came around the corner of the terrace from the living-room side, and looked over the edge.

'They're down there now, seeing to her, sir,' said the functionary. 'I'm afraid there's nothing at all to be done.'

Penk turned away. His face was set in an unfathomable expression.

'I guess she'll get all the attention she wanted now,' he said at last, then looked a little ashamed of himself as he saw his companion's face. 'I'm sorry. We'd better go in and lock the door. We don't want people staring. I'll get rid of everybody.'

'Perhaps we ought to take their names, sir. For the police, I mean.'

Penk stared at him.

'The police?' he said. 'Yes, they'll have to be called. Was it an accident? Did anybody see what happened?'

'Not as far as I know, sir. This terrace gives onto a back street, and there's not much traffic at this time of night. She was found by a group of passers-by.'

'Where did she fall from? This side of the terrace, it must have been. Did they see her fall?'

'No, sir. She was already lying in the street when they arrived. Nobody knows how long she had been there.'

There was a pause as Eugene Penk digested this.

'Let's go inside,' he said at last. 'I'll go downstairs and see to her. And we'd better tell Cora. That's her sister.'

They disappeared around the corner. Freddy waited a moment, then crept out through the door and looked over the railing. It was dark, but in the street six floors below he could just make out a group of people, who were gathered around something. Concerned voices floated up from below, while at intervals people left the group to fetch things, and others joined it. A blanket had been brought and draped over the figure lying in the street. Freddy grimaced, and began examining the wall and the railing that ran around the terrace. They were quite solid. Something fluttered in the corner of his eye, and he turned to see what it was. A tiny scrap of pink chiffon had caught on the railing. He bent to peer at it, but did not touch it. A table and chairs stood nearby, and he eyed the legs of the chairs, then shook his head. He looked down at his feet. The weather had been dry, so there were no traces of footprints to be had in that regard.

He was staring down into the street again when he felt a presence at his shoulder and saw that Corky Beckwith had come out onto the terrace through the same door, and was standing next to him. His face wore an expression that in anybody else Freddy would have described as akin to religious fervour.

'Dorothy Dacres dead!' he said, in a kind of ecstasy. 'Oh, the exquisite alliteration of it! It quite brings a tear to my eye. This will be a two-pager, at least! "Film star plummets to her death. Night of her greatest triumph." I only wish I'd been there to see it happen.'

'You really are a stinker, Corky,' said Freddy absently, for his attention was still directed towards the railing. From what he had seen, he did not like this at all.

He went back inside and into the living-room, where the guests were huddled in groups, looking about them as though waiting for somebody to tell them what to do. After the initial excitement, the news had finally begun to sink in, and everyone was speaking in solemn, hushed voices. Freddy was immediately accosted by Gussie, whose face wore an appalled expression.

'Oh, Freddy!' she cried. 'What an awful, awful thing! I can't bear it! And to think I'd just wished her dead. I'd take the words back this very minute if only I could.'

She threw herself into his arms and burst into tears. Freddy patted her gingerly on the back, conscious that Seymour Cosgrove was standing nearby, watching him with a hawk eye and scowling.

'There, there,' he said. 'Don't worry about it, old girl. It's just a figure of speech. I knew what you meant. You'd just had a disappointment, and anybody might have said that sort of thing in the heat of the moment.'

'That's all very well, but I shall feel terrible about it forever, I know I shall,' she said, sniffing. 'But how did it happen? Is the balcony safe? How did she come to fall? This is going to be the most dreadful scandal for the Abingdon. For all of us, in fact.'

'It's perfectly safe out there,' said Freddy. 'I've just been outside and had a look.'

'But then what happened? Did she jump?'

'I expect that's what the police will want to find out,' said Freddy. 'And here they are now, if I'm not much mistaken. Hallo, I know this one, don't I?'

A man in plain clothes but of unmistakably official appearance had just entered the room, in company with a police constable in uniform and another hotel functionary.

'Don't tell me they've called the Yard in already,' murmured Freddy to himself.

At a word from his senior, the police constable stationed himself by the door with a notebook, while the plain-clothes man surveyed the room. At last his eye fell on Freddy and he raised his eyebrows. Freddy disengaged himself gently from Gussie.

'Look, there's Mrs. Neale gaping at you,' he said. 'Go and tell her you're all right.'

'Oh, the poor dear,' said Gussie. 'She worries about me so, even when there's no need.'

She dried her tears and went off obediently, and Freddy approached the plain-clothes policeman.

'Hallo, Sergeant Bird,' he said. 'I'm sorry you missed the party. It was all going off nicely until a few minutes ago, but then someone decided to spoil the fun.'

'Hallo, Mr. Pilkington-Soames,' said Sergeant Bird. 'I didn't expect to see you here—although I suppose I might have known the papers would be sniffing around.'

'As a matter of fact, I'm not press this evening,' said Freddy. 'Or at least I wasn't until this happened. But I might just as well ask what you're doing here. It's not a Yard matter already, is it?'

'Not officially,' said Bird. 'The inspector and I were on our way back from somewhere else and just happened to catch the commotion in passing, so to speak. The constable over there was doing his best to keep order in the street, so we stopped to help him.'

'Entwistle's here, is he?'

'He's downstairs, directing operations, but he'll be up in a few minutes, once reinforcements have turned up. I'm under instructions to hold the fort here until he arrives. Who was the woman, then? They're saying downstairs it was Dorothy Dacres.'

'That's quite right,' said Freddy. 'Rather rude of her to leave in the middle of her own party, don't you think? Not exactly the done thing.'

Despite his words, his face was serious. The sergeant looked at him sharply.

'An accident, was it?'

'I don't think so. I can't see what she could possibly have been doing to overbalance and fall over the edge. The wall is three feet high and has a railing about fifteen inches high on top of it. She'd have to have been swinging on the thing to have tipped over it.'

'Drunk?' suggested Bird.

'It's possible, although she was certainly fairly sober earlier in the evening, as far as I could judge.'

'Suicide, then?'

'She'd just announced to a crowd of adoring fans that she was to play the starring rôle of a lifetime. Doesn't seem like the sort of thing that drives one to kill oneself, does it?'

'Not an accident and not suicide, you think? That only leaves one possibility,' said Bird.

'Yes, it does,' said Freddy. 'Of course, I'm not a detective, and I might be wrong.'

'Supposing you're not,' said the sergeant. 'Anyone in mind?'

Freddy thought of Gussie Lippincott, who had wished Dorothy Dacres dead only an hour earlier, and who had been mysteriously absent for several minutes before Dorothy's body had been discovered.

'She seems to have rubbed a lot of people up the wrong way,' he said at last. 'Half the people I've spoken to this evening had some grudge or other against her—even that little girl over there.'

'Is that so?' said the sergeant, regarding Adorable Ada, who at that moment was lolling on her mother's knee, half-asleep, with her thumb in her mouth.

'Yes. If it is murder, I should say you'll have your work cut out for you. But perhaps you'll find out it was an accident. I had a scout about just now and found the spot she fell from. She left a little scrap of her dress on the railing. I haven't touched it—that'll be for your chaps to examine.'

'Show me,' said Bird.

They went outside, and Freddy indicated the place from which Dorothy Dacres had presumably fallen. Corky Beckwith was still there, snooping about and peering over the railing.

'Ah, the police!' he said when he saw them. 'About time, too. Sergeant Bird, isn't it? I recognize you from the Hepton-stall case.'

'And who might you be?' said the sergeant, looking suspiciously at Corky's waiter's uniform.

'Oh, don't pay any mind to my attire—I happen to be in disguise this evening. Beckwith of the *Herald*, at your service. Tell me, what would you say if I told you this was all the fault of the demon cocaine, and that Dorothy Dacres threw herself from the balcony in a hallucinatory trance brought on by her fatal addiction to the drug?'

'I'd be most interested to hear it. Do you have any proof of this, sir?'

Corky waved his hand.

'Not proof as such, no,' he said. 'But the signs are all around you, sergeant. Just look at the rag-tag of people here tonight. I give you Pilkington-Soames as an example. Don't tell me he doesn't look distinctly seedy. And he's not the only one. I've had word from your department that someone has been supplying the stuff to these film people, and that's why I'm here this evening. If Dorothy Dacres wasn't a dope fiend, I'll eat my hat.'

'Do you know anything about this?' said the sergeant to Freddy.

'Not at all,' said Freddy, who had drunk less and behaved better that evening than perhaps on any evening that year. 'But I shouldn't listen to him too closely. The *Herald* has an obsession with this sort of thing.'

'I tell you—' began Corky, but the sergeant held up his hand.

'We shall hear your story in good time, sir,' he said. 'In the meantime, I'd better get back inside and wait for my inspector.'

As it happened, Inspector Entwistle had just arrived, in company with Eugene Penk. Dorothy's sister Cora was with them, too. She looked as though she had been crying. Entwistle glanced at Penk, who went to stand in the middle of the room and addressed the crowd in his carrying voice.

'I guess you've all heard there's been an accident tonight,' he said, as the guests fell silent. 'This was supposed to be a celebration, but I don't see much to celebrate right now. The police say you can all go home, but they're going to take everybody's names on the way out.'

He looked as though he wanted to say something more, but then shook his head grimly and walked off. One by one or in little groups the guests started to leave, and the constable at the door was kept busy writing as they filed out. At last only a few people remained. Robert Kenrick and his girl-friend had gone, as had Seymour Cosgrove. Basil and Birdie Kibble had left in a much subdued state, while the Neales had taken Gussie home, leaving Cora, Eugene Penk, and a silently crying maid to sit and stare at the detritus of the party. It would all have to be cleared away, but that would not be until tomorrow, for it was now long after midnight. Inspector Entwistle had inspected the terrace briefly, and had instructed one of the functionaries to lock the door. Cora and the maid would have to leave the suite, at least until the police had finished looking around, he said. The functionary was most sympathetic and accommodating. There was no other suite available, but the two ladies should both be made perfectly comfortable in rooms downstairs. Cora heard this without emotion. She seemed drawn and exhausted. Penk looked perpetually as though he wanted to say something, and opened his mouth frequently to begin, but each time he thought better of it and closed it again with a snap.

Corky and Freddy had remained behind too—Corky because he was determined that only brute force would remove him from the scene of such a story, and Freddy because he would have died rather than let Corky beat him. Inspector Entwistle regarded them impatiently.

'I said everyone out,' he said.

'Oh, but I can help you, inspector,' said Corky, full of self-importance. 'Thanks to this clever little disguise of mine, I've been the eyes and the ears of the place all evening, and I can tell you exactly what's been going on.'

'All in good time,' said Entwistle. 'Just leave your name with the man on the door, and you'll hear from us soon.'

'But—' said Corky.

'Out!' said Entwistle, and jerked his thumb towards the door.

Freddy saw it was time to leave.

'I'm sorry,' he said to Cora, and went out. After a little more sparring with the police, Corky followed him, and they went down together in the lift.

'I'm going to hang around here until they've finished scraping her up,' said Corky. 'It's just too late to get anything in for the morning edition, but I ought to make something rather good of it for the later ones.'

Freddy followed him half-unwillingly, but the body of Dorothy Dacres had already been removed, and there was little to be seen, apart from a police constable, who had been stationed there to discourage the curious. Corky went across and attempted conversation with the man, but was given short shrift.

'Nothing to be had there,' he said, returning to Freddy. 'Still, never mind. I have plenty of colour to put in. This is going to make the most marvellous story.'

And so saying, he departed. Freddy glanced around and up at the looming building. It was too dark to see much, six floors up, and he sighed. There was nothing to be done now, so he went home.

CHAPTER SEVEN

TRUE TO FORM, the *Herald* next day printed a lurid account, embellished with all kinds of 'facts' of dubious veracity, of the party at which Dorothy Dacres had died. The *Clarion*'s account was a much more muted affair, for that morning Freddy, somewhat to his puzzlement, had been summoned into the presence of Sir Aldridge Featherstone and instructed to tone it down.

'Why's old Feathers letting the *Herald* steal a march on us?' he said to Jolliffe at the next desk. 'This is a huge story, and he's letting them get away with the best of it.'

'Oh, didn't you know? He and Penk are in cahoots now,' said Jolliffe. 'Or at least, they will be soon. Sir Aldridge is to take a small share in Aston-Penk Productions and he's going to finance part of the film. I gather Henry Aston has been getting nervous about the whole business. It's quite a new enterprise, you know, and the first few pictures they made were awful flops, and he's been making noises about pulling out. Penk was here partly to look for some extra funds in case Aston finally gets cold feet and backs out of the whole deal. I say, I wonder whether Aston's heard about Dorothy Dacres. Do you think that will frighten him off once and for all?'

'If he has any sense he'll realize that the extra publicity can only be a good thing,' said Freddy. 'That's if the film goes ahead at all now it's lost its leading lady.'

'Oh, but I'm sure they can find someone else,' said Jolliffe. 'Film stars are two a penny nowadays. Weren't they talking about Augusta Laing for the rôle?'

'Yes,' said Freddy. He was thinking about the events of last night and wondering what the police had found out, if anything. At length he picked up the telephone and called Gussie. She was at home.

'Thank you, I'm much better today,' she said in reply to his inquiry. 'I did make rather a fool of myself last night, didn't I? Listen, why don't you come round? I've seen one or two reporters hanging about outside, and I need your help to chase them off, because I want to go and see Patience and chew on what happened last night. You must promise to be discreet, though. No printing it all in that rag of yours.'

'I promise I shall be as silent as the grave,' said Freddy.

Gussie was ready when he arrived, and came out to meet him.

'Have those awful men gone?' she said, glancing about. 'No, there's one of them now. He's been hovering outside all afternoon, making me nervous.'

'It's Clarkson from the *Bugle*,' said Freddy, then, as the man approached them, 'Do push off, there's a good fellow. Miss Laing doesn't want to talk to you.'

'Not today, at any rate, but thanks all the same,' Gussie added hurriedly. 'Might as well keep him sweet,' she whispered. 'You never know when I might need him.'

'I see you have a natural gift for this sort of thing,' said Freddy.

They found a taxi and jumped in.

'I haven't had a wink of sleep all night,' said Gussie, as the cab went through Russell Square. 'Poor Cora.'

Freddy noticed she did not say, 'Poor Dorothy.'

'I thought she and Dorothy didn't get along,' he said.

'Oh, they hated one another most of the time. I hate Pam and Vi half the time too, but that doesn't mean I shouldn't be devastated if something happened to either of them. That's how families work, isn't it?'

'Isn't Cora in films?' said Freddy.

'She was once, but didn't get very far, so gave it up. It's a shame, as she's every bit as pretty as Dorothy, and I heard she was very talented too. But Hollywood works in mysterious ways. They started out together, but Dorothy was the one who was championed by the studio Eugene Penk used to work for, and she's the one who became the star. It can't have been much fun for Cora to see her sister receiving all the attention while she struggled to get a contract, and so I imagine she stopped to save her pride in the end.'

'Was it Penk who championed Dorothy in the early days?'

'I don't know, exactly. I heard they had a prickly relationship, but he would certainly have had the power to make or break her career.'

'Then was it he who decided to give her the part of Helen Harper?'

'I suppose it must have been. He or Henry Aston, at any rate. I was thinking about it last night, and it suddenly came to me that it was all nonsense to start with—any hope of my getting the part, I mean. Ken wanted me, you see, and Penk wanted Ken, and so he strung him along until he'd agreed to direct the picture. Then once Ken had signed, Penk announced that Dorothy had got the part. I was never really in the picture at all.'

'You seem fairly cheerful about it, considering,' said Freddy. She gave him a sideways look.

'Of course I am,' she said. 'Last night I thought all was lost, but today—'

'Today?'

She hesitated, then suddenly gave him a brilliant smile.

'Well, let's just say things look a little brighter now,' she said.

'I see,' said Freddy, and relapsed into silence for the rest of the journey.

At the Neales' house all was in confusion, for Mrs. Neale had had the rugs taken up for beating, and furniture was piled up everywhere as maids scurried about busily. Kenneth Neale was barking down the telephone at someone called Lulu, who seemed to be a man, and from another room floated the sounds of Adorable Ada hammering out harmonic minor scales on the piano as though she meant to kill it. Every so often she would sing along in an operatic warble that sounded far too old for her.

'Oh, Augusta,' said Patience Neale when she saw them. 'Do excuse the mess. What about this dreadful business? What are they saying in the papers? I haven't had time to read them yet.'

'I shouldn't if I were you,' said Freddy. 'It's mostly fiction. To read it you'd be forgiven for thinking that the whole thing had happened in a Limehouse opium den.'

'But what happened? Did she jump, do you suppose? What do the police say?'

'I can't imagine it was suicide,' said Gussie. 'She was so beastly full of herself after the announcement that I can't think what would have made her miserable enough to take her own life an hour later—unless someone had just told her she had six weeks to live, or something.'

'Hardly likely, is it?' said Patience.

Kenneth Neale entered the room in his shirt sleeves and slippers.

'Well, I don't know what's going to happen now,' he said. 'I expect filming will have to be put back a while. I can't say I'm sorry for it, after what's happened. I'm having the solicitor go over the agreement, my dear, although he seems to think it will be water-tight. That'll teach me to believe the word of one of these Hollywood sharks again. Why, to think I let Penk fool me in that way! I thought I was wise enough not to fall for that sort of thing. Didn't I give him a piece of my mind! Of course, he made all kinds of excuses—said his hands were tied, and he'd done his best to get Aston to agree to casting Augusta, and that he'd made damn' sure she got the supporting rôle—but I didn't believe a word of it. I could hardly keep quiet when the silly Dacres woman was making that speech of hers, prattling about how much they wanted me for the picture, and how she was determined to prove herself worthy of me. Prove worthy of me! What do I care about a little has-been who hasn't made a decent picture in three years, and who couldn't act if her life depended upon it? I wanted someone who could do the job. I don't mind saying I could cheerfully have strangled her at that moment.'

'Careful, Ken, Freddy's press, you know,' said Gussie.

'Figure of speech, figure of speech,' said Neale hurriedly.

'Oh, don't mind me, sir,' said Freddy. 'I'm off duty. And you're not the only one to say something similar. I gather she'd put a few people's backs up lately.'

'Goodness, yes,' said Gussie. 'She snubbed Bob Kenrick's intended and went all out to draw him away from her, poor girl. She's obviously not used to these circles. Every time I saw her she looked as though she were trying not to cry. And Bob didn't seem too happy either. I think Dorothy had been throwing her weight about—you know the sort of thing: do as I say or I'll see to it that nobody will ever hire you in Hollywood. He's quite the coming thing, you know. Not the cleverest chap, perhaps, but he has tremendous screen presence, and I think Dorothy had some idea of hanging onto his coat-tails, since her career had been waning rather in recent years. I shouldn't be a bit surprised to find she'd tried to vamp him. Who else was there? Oh, yes—she was unkind to Ada, too.'

'It was most unnecessary,' put in Patience.

'And didn't Cora say something about her having lost Cosgrove his job?' said Freddy, remembering.

'Oh, Seymour,' said Gussie impatiently. 'He's impossible, but I suppose one ought to feel sorry for him. He's wanted to go to America for as long as I've known him, and I happen to know he needed the money urgently, too.'

'He must have been pretty sick when he found out that Dorothy had told them he wasn't coming,' said Freddy.

'Seymour, do you mean?' said a voice, and they turned to see Adorable Ada, who had stopped practising the piano and had come to see what the grown-ups were talking about. 'He wasn't happy at all, I think. I don't know what Dorothy did, but I overheard him talking to her last night. He was very angry and said he was going to kill her.'

'You mustn't repeat things like that, darling,' said Patience after a pause. 'And you oughtn't to have been listening to other people's conversations in the first place.'

'How can I help it if people stand next to me and talk?' said Ada. 'I can't shut my ears, can I?'

'A well-bred young lady would pretend not to have heard,' said Patience.

'Oh,' said Ada, and thought about this for a moment. 'Well, I shall know next time. Still, I think it was very *ill*-bred of them to talk in front of me as though I hadn't been there.'

She went out, and shortly afterwards began hammering on the piano again. Freddy looked after her thoughtfully, for he had just remembered the remark Seymour had made while Dorothy was announcing that she had got the part of Helen Harper. 'Someone's going to murder that woman one day,' Seymour had said. Had he been right?

CHAPTER EIGHT

S O IT WAS certainly cocaine, then?' said Sergeant Bird to Inspector Entwistle, who was reading a report.

'Looks like it,' said Entwistle. 'Not much of it—barely enough for half an hour's fun, in fact, but there's no getting away from it: Dorothy Dacres kept a small quantity of cocaine in a little silver box on her dressing-table.'

'What did Penk say about it?'

'Just about what you'd expect. He was all aghast and horrified, had no idea she was doing anything of the sort, wouldn't have dreamed of giving her the leading rôle in the film if he'd known, and so on and so on.'

'Think he was telling the truth?'

'Well, we've no proof he wasn't.'

'What about that sister of hers? Cora—what is it?—Drucker? Why not Dacres?'

'Oh, Dorothy Dacres wasn't her real name, of course. She was born Irma Drucker and changed it on the say-so of the studios. But the sister claims to have known nothing about the dope either, and swears Dorothy never touched it. We searched the place thoroughly while Cora and the maid were staying elsewhere, and we never found any drugs in among Cora's things—in fact, that little box was the only trace of the stuff we found, so for the moment I think we'll have to assume she's clean, and that Dacres was the only one who had anything to do with it.'

'What about this Beckwith fellow?' said Bird. 'He was there that night trying to dig up a story, and said he'd heard about the dope from our lot. Is that true?'

'It is true that the stuff's been turning up all over the place in London lately,' conceded Entwistle. 'You remember the case of Lord Menwith back in the summer. He wouldn't say where he'd got it, but it was obvious his wife was also heavily addicted—and a good few of his cronies, too, if I'm not much mistaken. Talbot's been put onto that. It's been making its way into high society somehow.'

'Carelli up to his tricks again?' suggested Bird.

'I shouldn't be surprised. We've found nothing on him or his associates, but they know we've been watching them so they've been extra careful. I expect this Beckwith has got his information from Talbot.'

'He certainly had a bee in his bonnet about it,' said the sergeant. 'He insisted Dorothy Dacres was a cocaine fiend and that she jumped off the terrace while under the influence.'

'Well, we'll soon find out when we hear from Ingleby,' said Entwistle. 'I told him to test for cocaine in her blood, and anything else he can find.'

'This other reporter, Pilkington-Soames, says she seemed sober enough to him at the party.'

'Yes—and what was he doing there, by the way?' said the inspector. 'Rather a suspicious coincidence, after all that funny business last month.'

'He's a friend of Augusta Laing's, he says, and wasn't working that evening. He didn't think much of the accident theory.'

'Well, he can keep his thoughts to himself,' said Entwistle.

'He was there on the spot, though, sir, and saw a lot of what was happening. He's right when he says that the railing was too high for her to have fallen over it accidentally. And suicide is most unlikely too; everyone we've spoken to says Dorothy Dacres was as happy as a sandboy that evening, and had no reason at all to kill herself—although I suppose it's always possible the cocaine gave her a brainstorm of some kind and drove her to do it.'

'Hmm, the drugs again,' said Entwistle. 'Well, we don't know yet that she'd actually taken any, so let's look at the rest of the facts.' He took out his notebook. 'Now, let's see: we know for certain that at half past ten or so Dorothy Dacres stood up and announced to everybody that she was to play the lead rôle in this film. As far as we can tell, she then spent the next twenty minutes sweeping around the room, demanding and receiving everybody's congratulations. But nobody seems to know where she went after that.'

'Presumably out on the terrace,' said Bird.

Entwistle looked back at his notes with a frown.

'She was found in the street at just before twenty past eleven by a group of passers-by, who raised the alarm. It seems that when they heard the commotion quite a lot of the guests upstairs rushed out to look over the railing, as they thought there'd been an accident in the street.'

He pursed up his mouth in distaste.

'Just curiosity I expect, sir,' said the sergeant. 'It's human nature, after all.'

'Not exactly pleasant, though. At any rate, we have half an hour or so in which we don't know what she was doing—or even where she was. We know she fell from the terrace, but we don't know for sure that she spent half an hour out there.'

'It seems unlikely,' said Bird. 'It was cold, and that evening-gown of hers was pretty flimsy.'

'We need to find out who was the last to see her alive,' said Entwistle, looking at the report again. 'Johnson said he couldn't find anyone who saw her go out onto the terrace. She spoke to a largish group of people at just before ten to eleven, then went off somewhere, and nobody seems to have seen her after that.'

'Did Johnson speak to all the guests?'

'Most of them. There were about a hundred people there and I asked him to eliminate the obvious ones. Many of them were nothing more than hangers-on, and didn't have much connection to the dead woman, or only spoke to her for a minute or two, but there are a few I dare say we'll want to speak to again. Let's see.' He paused a moment, referring again to his own notes. 'We may as well start with Penk,' he said at last. 'He seems to be the one in charge.'

'Who is this chap, anyway?' said Bird. 'Did he have some personal connection to Dorothy Dacres? Or was it purely business?'

'He's the head of Aston-Penk Productions—that's the studio that was going to make this film,' said Entwistle. 'I gather he'd come to England to woo a few people, too. He wanted to persuade Kenneth Neale to direct it—succeeded in that, it seems. Then there was Sir Aldridge Featherstone. Penk was hoping to get him to back this film and perhaps others. Now, who else have we? Cora again. She presumably knew her sister better than anyone.'

'I heard a rumour they didn't get on,' said Bird. 'Perhaps they had a row on the terrace and it ended in violence.'

'What, two little girls like that? I can't see them throwing each other off the top of a building, can you?'

'You'd be surprised at what women can do,' said the sergeant darkly. 'I've got two sisters, and some of the stories I could tell you would make your hair curl.'

Entwistle, who had no sisters, looked unconvinced.

'Anyway,' he went on after a moment, 'Miss Drucker says she hardly spoke to Dorothy at all that evening. She already knew her sister was getting the part, and so didn't need to congratulate her after the big announcement. She says she talked to various people, then went onto the terrace for a couple of minutes at about eleven, where she spoke to Robert Kenrick. A minute or two after that Miss Laing and Mr. Pilkington-Soames came out, then they all went inside.'

'Robert Kenrick was already on the terrace, was he?' said the sergeant with interest.

'Ah, I see that point struck you too,' said Entwistle.

'Do we know at what time he went out there?'

'He's a bit vague on the subject, but he claims he didn't speak to Dorothy at all after she made her grand announcement. He says he can't remember exactly what he did, but he wandered around the room talking to various people, then went outside for some fresh air.'

'Didn't he bring a girl with him to the party?' said Bird.

'Yes, he did, but it looks as though they didn't spend much of the evening together.' Entwistle glanced at the list of names. 'This is the one: Sarah Rowland.'

'Some falling-out there, do you think?' said the sergeant.

'Could be. I wonder whether Kenrick and Dacres were up to no good. You know what these actors are like—they hop from one to the next as easy as winking. I think we'll have to have a word with young Kenrick, and see what he has to say for himself.'

'He looks a likely one, if he was actually out on the terrace at around the time Miss Dacres died,' said the sergeant. 'Who else have we got?'

'Seymour Cosgrove,' said the inspector thoughtfully.

Bird threw his superior a keen glance.

'You like this one, do you, sir?'

'He's another very convenient suspect,' said Entwistle. 'He's a hot-headed chap, I understand, and by all accounts had a grudge against her, as she'd just lost him his job.'

'Did he tell you this?'

'No—Dacres herself told several people about it. Cosgrove was all set to go and work for one of these fashion magazines in America, but she wanted him as her own personal photographer, and so saw to it that he didn't. He was furious, but she thought it was all a huge joke.'

'Where was he that evening?' said the sergeant.

'He told Johnson he was around and about, talking to various people, but there are times we haven't been able to account for. There's one fifteen-minute period in particular, just after eleven o'clock, when nobody seems to have seen him. We'll have to look into that more closely. It would help if we knew at exactly what time she died.'

'It would certainly help us eliminate some of them,' agreed the sergeant. 'Or even all of them, assuming it wasn't deliberate at all, but suicide or an accident.'

'Whichever it was, we're going to have the devil of a job proving it,' said Entwistle.

'Leave it for the inquest to decide,' said the sergeant comfortably.

'Augusta Laing,' went on Entwistle. 'She'd just lost the part she wanted to Dorothy Dacres.'

'Did she take it badly?' said Bird.

'No—everyone says she took it very well, as a matter of fact. However, she's meant to be a good actress, so that might mean anything or nothing. She'd be able to hide her disappointment all right. Still, it's the same with her as with Cora. It would take some strength to chuck a full-grown woman off a balcony. That wall is high so you couldn't just push her over. I can't see a woman having done it, but we'll leave her on the list for now.'

'Any others?'

'Just Kenneth Neale, I think. He'd wanted Augusta Laing to play the part of Helen Harper—had only agreed to direct the film on that condition, in fact—so he was furious when the news was announced, and made no secret of it. He admits he followed Penk out onto the terrace and laid into him about it.'

'Oh, so they were out on the terrace too, were they?' said the sergeant.

'Not that terrace,' said Entwistle. 'They went onto the smaller one off Dacres' bedroom.'

'How long were they there?'

'It doesn't say here,' said the inspector. 'We'll have to do some more digging.'

'I should have thought Neale was furious with Penk, not Dorothy,' said Bird. 'He might have thrown Penk over the balcony, but not her.'

'True enough. But perhaps he talked to her afterwards and she angered him in some way. Anyway, those are the main suspects—if indeed we're looking for suspects. There's also Mrs. Neale, Sir Aldridge Featherstone, and these Kibbles, who were apparently singing at the piano all evening. Perhaps they can tell us more about what was going on.'

'Basil and Birdie,' said the sergeant reminiscently. 'I saw them at the Palais during the war. Very funny, they were.'

Entwistle scribbled a note or two.

'I wonder whether it *was* murder,' he said after a pause.

'It'll make our job a lot easier if it wasn't,' said Bird. 'I mean to say, if it turns out she'd had a skinful of cocaine then she might have tipped herself over the edge without anyone coming near her. "Temporarily unsound mind," they'd call it.'

'Yes. Perhaps you'd better get on to Ingleby, then,' said Entwistle. 'The sooner we find out whether she was taking the stuff, the better.'

CHAPTER NINE

FOR THE NEXT few days, the newspapers were full of the story of Dorothy Dacres' mysterious and tragic death, and theories abounded as to whether it had been an accident or something more suspicious. An inquest was opened and swiftly adjourned while the police gathered more evidence. Freddy was still under instructions to stick to the facts and avoid colouring his stories too highly, much to his exasperation.

'They're all in each other's pockets,' explained Jolliffe, who always seemed to be well informed about what was going on. 'Sir Aldridge has put up some cash for the production, and they don't want to scupper the thing now.'

'So the film is still going ahead, is it?' said Freddy.

'Sooner or later. Probably later, once they've found out who did the Dacres in and all the fuss has died down. It would look pretty callous to go ahead cheerfully with some other leading lady a week after the first one came a cropper, don't you think?'

'But what about Henry Aston? I thought he was getting skittish about the risk.'

'Penk's on the telephone to him most days, I hear,' said Jolliffe. 'He's managed to calm him down up to now, although I expect it will be touch and go. I suppose they're all hoping it'll turn out that she threw herself over the edge while drunk, or something like that. Then they can tidy it all away nicely and find some other pretty young thing to take the rôle of Helen Harper.'

'You seem to know a lot about it,' said Freddy.

'Oh, I hear it all from my mother. Lady Featherstone is her sister.'

'Is she, by George?' said Freddy, staring at Jolliffe in surprise and not a little consternation, remembering some of the disrespectful remarks about Lady Featherstone he had made in the past.

'Yes, didn't I mention it? That's how I got the job here. I keep it quiet as a rule, though, as some of the old boys back there like to mutter about nepotism.'

Freddy, who had got his job at the *Clarion* purely on the strength of his mother's influence, had nothing to say about that, and reverted to his original complaint.

'Well, it's dashed annoying, having my hands tied in this way,' he said. 'The *Herald* is having a high old time with it, of course. They're all fired up about this drugs aspect, even though no traces of anything were found in her body. If there's one thing Corky Beckwith loves more than a blonde dope fiend, it's a dead blonde dope fiend, and so you can be sure he's going to push that angle as hard as he can.'

'Oh, the *Herald*,' said Jolliffe dismissively, and went back to his work.

Freddy, however, was feeling distinctly disgruntled that, in spite of his having actually been there on the spot on the evening of Dorothy Dacres' death, he had been unable to take advantage of his inside knowledge and print any of the lurid rumours he had heard about the case. He was eager for more news, and so he decided to go and visit Gussie, to see if she had anything new to tell him. He had not got further than about halfway along Fleet Street, however, when he was accosted by Corky Beckwith himself, who was looking even more insufferably smug than usual.

'Well, isn't this just the most delightful coincidence,' said Corky, giving a smile that displayed to the full extent his uncommonly large helping of teeth. 'Here I was, wondering where you'd got to lately, and now here you are.'

'What do you want?' said Freddy grumpily.

'Why should you suppose I want anything? May we not walk together as allies in our chosen profession, comrades on the path of truth and justice, should our steps happen to be bent in the same direction for a furlong or two as we each plough our lonely furrow through life?'

'No,' said Freddy. 'Go and plough your furrow somewhere else and leave me alone.'

Corky gave a click of the tongue.

'Freddy, Freddy,' he said. 'It's obvious you're still smarting from the other day, and the *Herald*'s undeniably superior reporting on the Dorothy Dacres case. But you really oughtn't, you know. I mean to say, I'm rather older than you, and have been doing the job for longer, and experience will always show.'

He paused to reflect complacently on his grand and stately age of twenty-seven, and the worldly wisdom it had brought him. 'Still,' he went on kindly, 'that was really a nice little story you put together. I dare say a few people even read it. The *Clarion* does have one or two readers, I believe.'

'Do you have a point to make?' said Freddy. 'If not, I'd be most obliged if you'd push off. I'm in a hurry.'

'So I see,' said Corky, eyeing him speculatively. 'And where are you off to on this fine day? On the scent of a hot story, perhaps?'

'If I were I shouldn't tell you.'

'And I couldn't possibly expect it of you. Still, I did wonder whether you were going to visit one of your pals from the Abingdon. Miss Laing, for example?'

'Oh, it's *Miss Laing* now, is it?' said Freddy, walking faster to try and get rid of him. 'Have you run out of adjectives?'

'Not at all, not at all,' replied Corky, speeding up his own pace. 'But yes, perhaps I was a little—er—disrespectful earlier.'

'Look here, I haven't got time for this, so tell me what you want, then I can say no and be on my way, and you can go back to your office, or the Cheese, or wherever else they haven't barred you from yet. I expect there's a pig barn somewhere that will still admit you, if you slip them a couple of quid and promise to sit in the corner.'

'I shall ignore the ungracious tone of your voice,' said Corky, 'as I know perfectly well it conceals a brotherly affection for me that it's useless to deny, even to yourself. But listen,' he went on hurriedly at the sight of Freddy's exasperated expression, 'if you must know, I was hoping for a little *quid pro quo*.'

At the change in tone, Freddy looked up.

'What sort of *quid pro quo*?' he said suspiciously.

'Well, you know the *Herald* has been pursuing this angle about the cocaine that was found in Dorothy Dacres' room?'

'Yes, and to a degree that smacks almost of mania. What of it?'

'Just that I've been doing a little digging on the subject, with the help of my close friends at Scotland Yard. The police know the stuff has been coming in at Tilbury, and have intercepted a number of consignments. But it's not coming in in any sort of predictable way—I mean to say, one lot might arrive on a fishing-yawl from Rotterdam and another on a liner from Rangoon. Several people have been arrested, although obviously they're not talking—perhaps out of fear as to what will happen to them if they do. There's a rumour that the Carelli gang is behind it, since it all started earlier this year after Carelli himself got out of prison. I've been buzzing around, but it's difficult to get criminals to squeal to the papers, even for cash. A Beckwith never gives up, however, so I've started to look at it from the top end, as it were. That's why I'd been working at the Abingdon, you see—I'd heard there was a lot of that sort of thing going on there. But since you so ruthlessly forced me out of my honestly-obtained position at the hotel, I'm a little at a loose end, and so I was hoping we might embark upon a little partnership, you and I.'

'What exactly are you looking for?' said Freddy, interested in spite of himself.

Corky showed his teeth again, in what he hoped was an ingratiating smile.

'I want to find out how the dope is getting from Tilbury and into the hands of these people who ought to know better,' he said. 'It's a terrible problem, as I'm sure you're aware. Remember the case of Lord Menwith a few months ago? Such a terrible tragedy for a man of his stature, to be reduced to the gibbering simpleton we saw in court, don't you agree? Now, it's obvious that the low-lifes at the thick end of it all aren't being invited to society shindies to hand the white powder around on silver salvers, so it stands to reason that somebody high up must be dishing it out. I should like to find out who it is, and that's why I'm proposing we work together a little. None of these aristocrats will speak to me, you see.'

'I can't think why,' said Freddy, glancing askance at Corky, whose tailoring spoke of a devotion to frugality coupled with a desire to be visible in the dark.

'But you have an "in" on that sort of society, and if you can help me with that, then in return I shall help you with information about what's happening at the other end of the chain, so to speak. Just think of the splash we shall make if we find that the supplier is somebody important!'

'You've no evidence that anything in particular was going on that evening, though,' said Freddy. 'All we have is a little whiff of the stuff among Dorothy Dacres' things—and she might have got that at any time. There's no reason to think it was given to her that night. I think you're barking up the wrong tree.'

'No, no, no,' said Corky. 'I have a feeling about this in my bones. I believe the person in question was at the party that night, and once we find out who it was, we'll know who killed Dorothy Dacres. Shouldn't you like to catch her murderer?'

'What makes you think it *was* murder?' said Freddy, although privately he was of the same opinion.

'Oh, but of course it was! It's too beautiful a story for it not to have been,' said Corky. 'And even if it wasn't, that hardly matters. There's enough copy to stretch the story out for weeks if we use it wisely. Admit it, it does seem very suspicious, don't you think?' he went on hurriedly, seeing Freddy's face. 'And it all makes perfect sense. Why, look at what we know: Dorothy Dacres uses coke, and the very night I turn up looking for it, she falls off a balcony.'

'Isn't that a coincidence?'

'No,' said Corky. 'I believe somebody recognized me and decided to take action against the only person who could expose him.'

'Full of yourself, aren't you?' said Freddy. 'You're not seriously suggesting that your mere presence struck terror into the heart of some person unknown, and drove him to murder? If you didn't recognize him, then how is it that he recognized you?'

'Because my name is known and feared among the unrighteous of our great city,' said Corky. Freddy snorted, and he went on, 'Well, then, even if it wasn't I who spurred him into heinous action, perhaps it was Dorothy Dacres herself. Perhaps she threatened to expose him, and he threw her off the terrace as a warning to others.'

They had now reached Aldwych. Freddy had intended to take the Underground, but he suspected that Corky meant to follow him all the way to Gussie's house, and so he started looking about for a taxi instead.

'Look here, this is all bunk,' he said. 'You've taken a piece of evidence that might not have anything to do with her death, and built it up into I don't know what.'

'Then you won't help me?'

Freddy knew Corky of old, and knew there was an even chance that not a word of his story was true. Still, he did not want Corky to get the scoop either, and so he decided to hedge his bets.

'Your story is too vague,' he said. 'Stuff coming in at Tilbury, indeed! Why, I could have found that out myself if I'd wanted to. Come and see me again when you've found out something useful, and then perhaps we can come to an arrangement. Until then there's nothing doing, I'm afraid.'

'Hmph,' said Corky. 'Think you're the smart one, don't you? But I can see what you're at. You want me to provide you with all the information so you can step in at the last minute and claim the glory. Well, you'd better not try anything funny. This story is mine, and I'm only letting you in on it as a favour.'

'You're letting me in on it because you don't have anything, and you want me to do all the work for you,' said Freddy, and got into a taxi. As it departed, he saw Corky looking after him with a calculating expression upon his face.

Chapter Ten

CORA DRUCKER SAT in a peach satin-upholstered arm-chair, watching Inspector Entwistle as he walked around the living-room of the penthouse suite at the Abingdon, taking everything in. Sergeant Bird was observing quietly from the corner.

'I beg your pardon for the interruption, Miss Drucker,' the inspector said after a minute or two, 'but it's looking increasingly likely that your sister's death was not an accident, and so it's vital we find out exactly who spoke to Miss Dacres and when on the evening in question.'

'I quite understand,' said Cora dully, her arms folded in front of her body.

'I don't want you upsetting Cora,' said Eugene Penk, turning round from where he had been gazing out onto the terrace. He, too, seemed subdued, and most unlike his usual ebullient self. It was five days since Dorothy Dacres had died, and he was becoming restless. He hated any period of enforced inactivity, but was unable to continue with business while the cause of his leading lady's death remained unresolved.

'Don't worry about me, Eugene,' said Cora. 'I just want to find out what happened. Poor Dorothy! I knew it wasn't suicide—she was far too happy for that—but I could have believed in an accident. But now it seems it wasn't even that.'

'Not unless she climbed onto the railing and overbalanced,' said Entwistle. 'And that's not very likely. She might have stood on a chair, but there was none standing near the edge at the time.'

'Are you sure of that?' said Penk. 'Someone might have moved it back afterwards.'

'We had a close look at them all,' said Entwistle, 'and it was clear that none of them had been moved for several weeks, from the dirt and dead leaves that had piled up around the legs.'

'Then you think she was pushed over?' said Cora.

'It looks very possible,' said Entwistle. 'That's why we need to find out who was doing what in the half an hour between ten to eleven, when she was last seen alive, and twenty past, when she was found in the street.'

'The other policeman asked me that,' said Cora. 'As far as I recall, I was in here most of the time. I know I was looking for Bob Kenrick, as I wanted to speak to him about something. I think I must have asked everyone at the party whether they'd seen him, but I eventually found him on the terrace at about eleven. He'll tell you. Then Augusta and her friend came out and we spoke for a minute and then went back indoors. That must have been at ten past eleven. Then I went to find Dorothy but nobody knew where she was, so I talked to Lady Featherstone instead. We were still talking when Eugene came and told me the news. We had to go downstairs and identify her.'

This last was said in a whisper. She blinked and her face worked, but she quickly mastered herself.

'I'm sorry to have to remind you of it,' said Entwistle. 'But I'm sure you understand that we have to ask the questions.'

'I understand perfectly,' she said. 'Please carry on.'

'When you went outside, it was onto the main part of the terrace, outside the living-room?' said Entwistle.

'Yes.'

'And you didn't go around the corner, to the part that leads off your bedroom, at any time?'

'No. That's where Dorothy fell from, I guess?'

'Most likely, yes,' said the inspector. 'Then you were in the living-room and on the main part of the terrace all the time?'

'I think so. I talked to quite a few people, so they can probably confirm it.'

'Oh, but you weren't,' said Penk suddenly. 'I was on the second terrace with Neale for a while, and you came out and saw us, don't you remember?'

'Of course,' said Cora, thinking. 'That was just for a moment, though. I thought Bob might be with you.'

'You went onto the other terrace? At what time was that?' said Entwistle.

'Why, it must have been at about five to eleven, I think. Yes, it was, because I remember thinking after that that I'd tried one terrace and the only place left to look was the other.'

'Very well,' said Entwistle. 'Now, what about you, Mr. Penk? You say you went out onto the smaller terrace outside Miss Dacres' bedroom. At what time was that?'

Penk considered.

'Ten to eleven, or thereabouts,' he said at last. 'I can't be exact, but it must have been around then, because I was one of the people talking to Dorothy until just before she disappeared. We made the tour of the room together, because everybody wanted to congratulate her, and I was by way of being responsible for giving her the part, so it seemed we might as well give everybody the chance to talk to us both at once. And I don't mind admitting I was trying to avoid Kenneth Neale,' he added humorously. 'I knew he would be mad at me about the whole thing, so I stuck by Dorothy for protection.'

'Why did you think he would be mad at you?'

'Because he wanted Augusta Laing to play Helen Harper. I wanted Neale to direct the picture, so I'd given him the impression that she'd got the part—or at least, let's say I didn't contradict him—but I thought he'd come around to the idea once he saw what Dorothy could do.'

'Didn't you want Miss Laing for the part?' said Entwistle.

Penk gave an expressive shrug.

'As a matter of fact, I did,' he said, 'but it wasn't my decision to make. I'm only a part-owner of Aston-Penk Productions—and that's the smallest part. You've heard of Henry Aston. He's the top dog in this partnership, and what he says goes.'

'Do you mean he makes all the artistic decisions?'

'No,' said Penk. 'He gives me my head for the most part, but if he wants to override me then there's not much I can do about it. He's the money.'

'Even if it's bad business?'

'Henry's not his father. He inherited millions, and he's casting about, wondering what to do with them. Give him a shipyard or a railroad and he's on firm ground, but he's not so sure of himself with movies. He's got the bug, though, and he was determined to invest—and I was hardly going to say no to the money. But the company's still young, and finding its feet, and we've made a couple of pictures that didn't do so well, so Henry didn't want this one to go badly. He wanted a big star for this one—and Dorothy was certainly that, so I went along with it. It's not the best way to run a business, I know, and as a matter of fact, part of the reason I came to London was to speak to someone else who was interested in backing the venture.'

'Sir Aldridge Featherstone?' said Entwistle.

'Yes. The idea was that if we had more investors, Henry would be less nervous and more inclined to let me make the decisions. We'll see if it succeeds.'

'So,' said the inspector, consulting his notes. 'You were with Miss Dacres and a crowd of other people until about ten to eleven. Did you see where she went after that?'

'No, because then Kenneth Neale grabbed hold of me and demanded my attention—said he wanted to speak to me. I thought I might as well get it over and done with, so we went into Dorothy's room and out onto the little terrace.'

'Was anybody else there?'

'No—and a good thing too! Neale wasn't at all happy, and bawled me out in no uncertain terms. I listened to him as long as I could—thought it was best to let him get it off his chest. Then I gave him the soft soap a little, and said that Augusta was going to be a big star, there was no doubt about that, and that we'd give her a lot of publicity and put her first in line for any other plum parts that came up. He was muttering about having his lawyer look over his contract, but I calmed him down all right, and said we'd talk about it another time and see what could be done, then he went away. I stayed outside for a few minutes—I wanted a little peace and quiet after all that, so I smoked a cigar, then came back into the living-room. Then I heard people saying there'd been an accident, and, well—'

He tailed off and was silent for a moment. Then he glanced at Cora.

'I think I'd better tell them,' he said.

Cora looked surprised.

'Tell us what?' said Entwistle.

'It would only come out sooner or later,' said Penk, still addressing Cora. He sighed. 'Dorothy and I were married, inspector.'

The two policemen glanced up quickly, and Penk went on:

'In name only, lately. We married ten years ago, when she was just starting out in Hollywood. We kept it quiet for the good of her career, as I'd just been through an unpleasant divorce from my first wife, and the public doesn't like its stars to get caught up in that kind of thing. We didn't want them to get the idea that she was the other woman. Then after that, we started putting Dorothy in ingénue parts, and she wanted to play up to that image—after all, it wouldn't have looked quite right for her to have been married to a man nearly twenty years older than she. The studio sent her out on the town to be photographed with young actors, and we kept it hidden very well. We always planned to come out with it sooner or later, but after a few years the marriage failed and then there seemed no sense in telling everybody.'

'There was no divorce?' said Entwistle.

'Not yet,' said Penk. 'We planned to do it, but we hadn't gotten around to it yet. She said she was going to file when she got back to the States.' He laughed bitterly. 'Now it's too late.'

'And yet you remained on good terms?'

'Yes, mostly,' said Penk. 'She was a difficult woman—there's no denying it—but we got along well enough professionally. I wouldn't have mentioned it, except that you'd have dug it up in the end anyhow. But I don't see it changes anything about her death.'

'Perhaps not,' said Entwistle, who was thinking. At present he could not see it made much difference, but it was a surprising new fact that must be added to the collection of other facts.

'This substance we found in Miss Dacres' room,' he began.

At that, Cora shook her head.

'I told you, I don't know anything about it,' she said. 'She never did anything like that, and I don't know what she was thinking. If you ask me, it belonged to someone else. Maybe she was keeping it for them. And it wasn't for me, if that's what you're thinking,' she added. 'I've never touched the stuff.'

'Cora's right,' said Penk. 'I think she was holding it for a friend. Perhaps she didn't even know what it was.'

'Well, we didn't find any traces of cocaine in her blood,' said Entwistle, non-committally. 'However, I should very much like to find out where she got it, since it might well prove to have been a motive for murder.'

Penk and Cora stared at one another blankly.

'Murder,' said Cora at last. 'It's such a terrible word. How could anybody have murdered Dorothy? I can't believe it.'

'You mean nobody had reason to kill her?' said Entwistle. 'Did she have no enemies at all?'

She hesitated.

'Everyone has enemies in this business,' she said. 'Dorothy was difficult, right enough, but I don't know why anybody would go so far as to kill her.' She shivered. 'I just wish we knew what really did happen that night.'

'That's what we mean to find out,' said Entwistle.

CHAPTER ELEVEN

'THIS MARRIAGE PUTS a new aspect on things,' said Entwistle, as they left the Abingdon. 'Although I'm not quite sure how.'

'No,' agreed Bird. 'It might have been one thing if she'd been sneaking off with other men behind his back, but if they weren't living as man and wife any more it doesn't make much of a motive. I mean to say, I don't suppose he'd have been very pleased about it, but he'd hardly be jealous enough to kill her.'

'That's if he was telling the truth. We can easily confirm his story about the marriage, but proving they were amicably separated is another matter.'

'You think he might have been lying about that?' said Bird. 'She was supposed to have had her eye on Robert Kenrick, wasn't she? I suppose Penk might have killed her in a jealous rage, then, if she was displaying it a bit too openly at the party that night—oh, but he was on the second terrace for most or all of the time in question, so it looks as though he's let out.'

'He *says* he was on the second terrace all that time, but can he prove it? He might have sneaked across to the other one and done it while nobody was watching.'

'Well, he'd have had to come through the living-room to do it, so if he did then somebody is bound to have seen him,' said the sergeant. 'And it looks as though Miss Drucker is out of the picture, too, since she was talking to one person or another—including Robert Kenrick—for the whole half-hour.'

'Ah, yes,' said Inspector Entwistle. 'Now, Kenrick had the most opportunity of all of them, since he was out on the main terrace for a large part of the fatal period. Let's see what he has to say for himself.'

They found Robert Kenrick at his flat in Knightsbridge. It was large and spacious, and had the messy, unfurnished appearance of having been recently acquired. Although it was late morning, he was still in his dressing-gown, with rumpled hair, but he admitted them readily enough—and indeed, when they entered the living-room they found that they were not the first visitors to arrive, for another man was lounging comfortably on a sofa, smoking.

'I expect you recognize Basil,' said Kenrick. 'Basil Kibble, you know.'

In broad daylight, without his make-up, Basil Kibble appeared far closer to his real age, for he had the pale, unhealthy look and bloodshot eyes of a man who spends little time in the open air, and goes late to bed every night. His suit was worn and shabby, with shiny patches at the elbows, and altogether his daytime appearance was a far cry from the elegant and sophisticated *persona* he affected during his evening performances.

'Hallo, inspector,' he said cheerfully, without moving. 'I'm here to cheer up the patient. Ought I to get up? Or might we dispense with the formalities? Should you prefer me to leave altogether, in fact?'

'No need, sir,' said Entwistle. 'I believe you and your wife were at the Abingdon on the night Miss Dacres died?'

'Oh, we were, we were,' said Basil. He lowered his voice and looked suitably sombre. 'Terrible thing to happen, and on such a triumphant night for her. I suppose you're here to question Bob. Shall I go out of the room, dear boy? I can be as discreet as you like.'

'No, no, I'd rather you stayed,' said Robert Kenrick. 'You might remember things I don't. As a matter of fact, I'd much prefer to forget the evening entirely, but I don't suppose I'll be allowed to.'

'Oh? Was Miss Dacres a particular friend of yours?' said Entwistle.

'No,' said Kenrick shortly. Basil shot him a warning glance, and he continued hastily, 'That is to say, I didn't know her well. We'd only met a week or two earlier.'

'And there was no closer connection between you than that?'

'If you mean were we having an affair, then the answer is no,' he said. 'I'm engaged—or I was, at any rate.'

'That would be to Miss Sarah Rowland,' said Entwistle. 'She accompanied you to the party that evening.'

'Yes,' said Kenrick suddenly. 'And I wish we hadn't gone, because she hasn't spoken to me since.'

'Why not?'

Kenrick opened his mouth to answer, but again there was the warning look from Basil Kibble, and he closed it again.

'We had a row,' he said at length. 'It was a private matter that had nothing to do with what happened that night.'

'Are you certain of that?' said Entwistle. 'Your fiancée wasn't, perhaps, upset because she suspected you of having deserted her for Miss Dacres?'

'No,' said Kenrick, but his tone was unconvincing. For an actor, he did not seem very good at dissembling.

The inspector went on:

'Several people observed that evening that Miss Dacres seemed to be taking an unusually close interest in you. It was also noted that she snubbed Miss Rowland publicly, and that Miss Rowland was upset, and spent most of the evening sitting in a chair at one side of the room.'

'It was all nonsense,' said Kenrick. 'I told Sarah that, but she didn't believe me. This is all new to her—it's new enough to me, too—and she doesn't feel quite comfortable among this sort of people yet. This was the first time she'd met any of them, and most of them were friendly enough, but then Dorothy came and thought she'd try to lord it over me in front of everyone. I had to play along a little—for the sake of the publicity, you know. One has to keep up a certain image. But Sarah didn't like it one bit.'

'What do you mean by play along? Do you mean you took part in the pretence that there was a romance between you and Dorothy?'

'Not exactly,' he replied uncomfortably. 'We pretended to flirt—or at least, I let her flirt with me, because Sarah was looking daggers at us both.'

'And there was nothing on your side?'

'Not at all.'

'What about Miss Dacres? Can you be sure it was all just for show?'

'Ye-es,' said Kenrick.

'You don't seem quite certain.'

'I didn't mean a thing to her, I'm sure of it,' said Kenrick unwillingly.

'But—' prompted Entwistle.

Kenrick cast a glance at Basil Kibble as though in entreaty.

'Don't look at me,' said Basil. 'You know what I thought of her. Inspector, what Bob is far too much of a gentleman to tell you is that Dorothy Dacres was badgering the life out of him.'

'Is that true?' said the inspector.

Kenrick looked embarrassed.

'She made a suggestion,' he said at last. 'She said it would help our careers if people thought we were really—you know. And it would be good publicity for the picture.'

'And what did you say?'

'I was flattered, naturally, and I told her so, but I said I already had a girl and couldn't think of it.'

'How did she take it?'

'Why, she had to accept it,' he said with finality.

'She wasn't upset?' said Entwistle.

'No.'

'She didn't perhaps threaten you, or tell you she'd see to it you were fired from the picture?'

'No, of course not. Who told you that?'

'One or two people had that impression,' said Entwistle vaguely.

'Well, it's not true,' said Kenrick.

'Very well, then. Let's turn to the events of the party. We are trying to discover the circumstances behind Miss Dacres' death, and to do that we need to know what she was doing immediately before she fell from the terrace. There is a period of about half an hour in which nobody seems to have seen her, and we'd like to know where she was and what she was doing during that time. Now, we know that at half past ten she announced to everybody that she had won the part of Helen Harper, and after that she spent a little while circulating and accepting congratulations. But we don't know exactly where she was after about ten to eleven—although obviously we can assume she went out onto the terrace at some point. Did she go out with you?'

'No,' said Kenrick.

'And yet you were on the terrace for some time after half past ten.'

'Was I? Yes, I suppose I was.'

'At what time did you go out there?'

'I—I don't know. I wasn't particularly paying attention.'

'Was it after Miss Dacres made the announcement, or before?'

'Why, I—after, I think it must have been. Yes, it was. She mentioned me in her speech, I remember.'

'Did you go outside immediately after she'd finished speaking?'

'I spoke to a few people, I think. They wanted to congratulate me on getting the part in the film, so of course one had to go along with things and seem pleased, although I didn't feel much like it.'

'What did you do on the terrace?'

'Nothing. Sarah wouldn't speak to me and I was feeling pretty down and didn't want to talk to anybody, so I suppose I looked out at the view and smoked.'

'You didn't think of going home?'

'No, I didn't, although I expect I ought to have. But I was there as the leading man, and I didn't want to offend anybody.'

'I see,' said Entwistle. 'Then you stood there on the terrace the whole time. Did you stay in one place?'

'Yes.'

'You didn't go around the corner to the other side of the terrace at any time?'

'No.'

'Did you speak to anybody or see anybody?'

'Not at first. Cora came out after a while, and we talked for a minute or two, but she was a little distracted and seemed to be waiting for somebody.'

'Who was that?'

'Augusta, I think. She fairly ran over to her when she and her chap came outside. Then I realized how cold it was and went back indoors.'

'You went inside before Miss Drucker?'

'Yes.'

'At what time was that?'

'I don't know. Perhaps Cora or Augusta will remember. I left the three of them on the terrace.'

'And what did you do after that?'

'Nothing much,' said Kenrick. 'Talked to one or two people, I think.'

'You didn't go back out onto the terrace at all? Perhaps through Miss Drucker's bedroom?'

'Certainly not. I'd got cold and wanted to stay where it was warm.'

'When did you realize Miss Dacres was dead?'

'Not until I heard the commotion and Penk started charging around, yelling at people to get off the terrace. A lot of people had rushed outside because they thought there'd been a motor accident, and Penk shouted at them to get back in. Then everybody started whispering that it wasn't a car crash after all—that Dorothy had fallen from the terrace. After that the police arrived, and it was obvious we were in the way, so we gave our names to the constable on the door and I took Sarah home. That was an uncomfortable journey, I can tell you. Now every time I telephone, her mother answers and won't let me speak to her.'

'Poor old chap,' said Basil. 'Give it another day or two and I'm sure she'll come round.'

Kenrick said nothing, but looked glum. Entwistle turned to Basil Kibble.

'I don't suppose you remember what you were doing during the half-hour in question?' he said.

'Oh, Birdie and I were on duty, inspector,' replied Basil. 'In every house you'll always find us at the piano. I'm sure you'll have no difficulty in finding people to confirm that.'

'Very well,' said Entwistle. 'I think that will be all.'

'Tell me, do you have an inkling of what happened that night?' said Basil. 'I gather from others you've been bustling about asking people to give alibis. But what if it was an accident?'

'Then we still need alibis to prove that,' said the inspector. 'If nobody was with her at the time, then everyone is cleared of suspicion, and we can safely say she died by her own hand one way or another.'

'In that case, I have no more to say,' said Basil. 'I wish you the best of luck—and all the more so, because I think you're going to need it.'

Chapter Twelve

———

'ARE WE SURE it wasn't an accident?' said Sergeant Bird, once they were out in the street.

'No, we're not,' said Inspector Entwistle. 'But there's no reason in the world I can see that Dorothy Dacres should have climbed up onto the railing and fallen over. She was reasonably sober by all accounts, and certainly had no reason to throw herself over deliberately.'

'Horseplay?'

'That's always possible, but then surely somebody must have been there with her. Why would she have been fooling about by herself?'

'True,' said Bird. 'So, then, who do you fancy? This Robert Kenrick doesn't seem to have much of an alibi.'

'No—he was on the terrace alone for some of the time in question—or so he says—and it sounds as though he had a motive, too. He didn't want to make too much of it, but it's obvious Dorothy Dacres had been pestering him, and perhaps threatening him. He's at the beginning of his career, and she was a powerful woman with some influence. Perhaps he decided to put her out of the way to make her stop bothering him. Still, at the moment we don't have enough evidence to arrest him, as there's nothing to connect him with the crime, or the accident, or whatever it was.'

'No, it's all pretty flimsy,' agreed Bird. 'Not a jury in the land would convict him on the strength of a missing alibi—he's far too good-looking. Now, who's next on our list?'

Entwistle looked at his watch.

'The super wants to see me at two and it's getting late, so I think we'd better split up. I'm going to go and speak to Seymour Cosgrove. You can go and try Sarah Rowland. She was sitting down for most of the evening, and there's nothing like a scorned woman for watching the former object of her affections like a hawk. If anybody can tell us what Robert Kenrick was doing during that half an hour, she can.'

'Right you are, sir,' said the sergeant.

'And she lives with her mother, too, who I gather is a bit of a tartar. You're better at worming your way around that sort than I am. Go and see if Miss Rowland is at home, and I'll see you back at the Yard later.'

So they parted, and Sergeant Bird headed for Bayswater, where Robert Kenrick's fiancée lived with her mother. Sarah Rowland had given her profession as teacher, so Bird hardly expected her to be at home, and was therefore not surprised when the door was answered by a woman of fifty or so, who on inquiry proved to be Miss Rowland's mother. Bird had been expecting a dragon, but she was very small and smartly dressed, with iron-grey hair and a determined chin.

'Oh, police,' she said, when Sergeant Bird introduced himself. 'Yes, Sarah is at home.'

'Who is it?' said a voice behind her, and a young woman appeared. She was small, like her mother, and delicately pretty, with a pale face.

'I'd like to ask you some more questions about the party at the Abingdon Hotel last week, if you don't mind,' said Bird.

Sarah Rowland glanced at her mother, who folded her lips.

'Very well, you'd better come in,' she said.

They went through to a small parlour furnished in the style of a few years ago. On a table by a wall, papers and exercise books were spread out.

'It's a field day today,' said Miss Rowland, by way of explanation. 'I'm not wanted so I stayed at home to do a little extra work.'

Mrs. Rowland seemed inclined to hover.

'Don't worry—I shall be quite all right,' said Sarah, and after a brief glance at Sergeant Bird, the older woman left the room. 'Mother is rather protective,' said Sarah. 'She means well, but sometimes she goes a little too far.'

'Better safe than sorry,' said Bird. 'And she's been doing her job well, according to Mr. Kenrick.'

Sarah Rowland stuck out her chin, and at that moment looked very like her mother.

'Have you come to plead his case?' she said.

Sergeant Bird might have pointed out that he was a Scotland Yard detective, not a match-maker, but he did not.

'No, not at all,' he said. 'I'm here as part of our inquiry into the death of Miss Dorothy Dacres.'

'Was she killed deliberately?' said Sarah.

'That's what we'd like to find out.'

'I shouldn't be surprised if she had been,' she said.

'Oh? Why is that?'

'Because from what I've heard of her, she was the sort to trample over everybody who stood in her way—a sort of bully, I suppose. And sometimes bullies can go too far, and one day they find that those they have tormented won't stand for it any more.'

'Do you think that's what happened?' said the sergeant. 'You think she was killed by somebody she'd offended?'

'I don't know,' said Sarah hesitantly. She seemed suddenly to have realized the implications of what she was saying.

'Do you think she was bullying Mr. Kenrick?' said Bird.

'No—that is—'

'Miss Rowland, I wanted to speak to you particularly because I understand you were sitting down for much of the evening, and in a position to observe everything that happened. Now, we don't know whether Miss Dacres died accidentally or whether she was killed deliberately, and the only way we are likely to find out is by ascertaining what each of the guests was doing at the time of her death.'

'You think Bob did it, don't you?' said Sarah suddenly.

'Why do you say that?'

'Because he was out on the terrace just before she died.'

It looked as though Inspector Entwistle had been right in his supposition that Miss Rowland had been watching Robert Kenrick carefully all evening.

'He has admitted he was there, yes,' said Bird.

'He can admit it all he wants, but I can tell you now that he didn't kill her, because he's simply incapable.'

'Can you be quite sure of that?' said the sergeant gently.

'Of course I can. I won't deny I'm angry with him, but it's not for the reason you might think. I know perfectly well there was nothing between Bob and Dorothy Dacres. I could see the kind of woman she was as soon as I met her, but I'd suspected it even before that, from some of the things Bob said. She was all out for herself, and woe betide anybody who got in her way.'

'I see,' said Bird. 'And you are angry with Mr. Kenrick because he didn't stand up to her, is that it?'

'Yes,' said Sarah. 'It was positively exasperating to see it. I know what he's like, sergeant. He is the sweetest-tempered man you could ever hope to meet, and I love him for it, but it does mean that he is terribly easily taken advantage of. He's supposed to be going to Hollywood soon, and I fear for him. He has the talent, but I'm so very afraid the studios will crush him.'

'Perhaps he needs you to protect him,' said Bird.

'Perhaps. But I'm dreadfully cross with him at the moment for allowing himself to be put in such a difficult position. And now it's become even more difficult, because everybody thinks he killed Dorothy.'

'Suppose you tell me what else you saw that evening,' said the sergeant. 'It may be that you can help prove he had nothing to do with it.'

'Very well,' she said. 'What do you want to know?'

'Where were you when Miss Dacres made the announcement that she'd been given the part of Helen Harper? Were you still sitting down?'

'Yes.'

'Where was your chair, exactly?'

'Near the wall, behind the piano and to one side.'

'Then you must have had a good view of everything that was going on.'

'Yes, I suppose I did.'

'Can you tell me what you remember about the period after Miss Dacres made her announcement? What did you see?'

Miss Rowland thought for a moment.

'Well, there was a lot of cheering and clapping when she said she'd got the part, although one or two people didn't seem too pleased about it. The director—Kenneth Neale, I think his name is—looked particularly surprised and annoyed. But I've found out since then that he was expecting Augusta Laing to get the part.'

'How did Miss Laing look? Do you remember?'

'I wasn't watching her, so I couldn't tell you.'

'Then what happened?'

'Dorothy grabbed Mr. Penk by the arm and did a sort of tour of the room so that people could congratulate her.'

'Where was Mr. Kenrick then?'

'Oh, he was receiving congratulations too, as she'd announced him as the leading man. He'd been grumpy all evening after we fell out, but that cheered him up a bit. Then he came across to me, but I'm afraid I turned away from him and wouldn't speak to him, so he stalked off in a huff. Then I saw him go out onto the terrace.'

'At what time was that?'

'About a quarter to eleven, I think. Yes—it must have been then, because I remember glancing at my watch and wondering whether I should get home before midnight.'

'When did he come back in?'

'I don't know, exactly. Perhaps just after eleven.'

'What did he do after that?'

'I don't know. There was a little crowd of people standing between us for a moment, and when they dispersed I couldn't see him any more. I didn't see him again until all the shrieking began.'

'So for a good while Mr. Kenrick was not in view. What did you do while he was absent?'

'Watched everybody else, I suppose.'

'Tell me what you saw. Where did Miss Dacres go, for example?'

'Why, I don't quite know. She was awfully full of herself, of course, and sailed around the room with Mr. Penk for a while as though she owned the place. Then Kenneth Neale came and took Mr. Penk away from her, and the two of them went through a door—I think into Dorothy's bedroom. I got the impression they wanted to talk in private. Then—I'm not sure—I remember Miss Drucker caught hold of Dorothy and whispered something to her, which seemed to make her puff up even more, but I don't know where she went after that.'

'Did she go somewhere with Miss Drucker?'

'Oh, no. They only talked for a second, in passing.'

'You say Mr. Penk and Mr. Neale went into Dorothy's room. At what time did they come out?'

Sarah frowned.

'Mr. Neale came out at about eleven,' she said at last.

'Can you be sure of that?' said Bird.

'Yes, I can,' she said, 'because he came out and spoke to his wife and mentioned going home, and I looked at my watch again.'

'And what about Mr. Penk?'

'He came out just as the man from the hotel arrived,' she said. 'Then he started charging about and ordering people off the terrace.'

'He didn't come out at all before that?'

'No,' she said. 'I'm sure I'd have seen him. I was practically facing the door to Dorothy's room, you see.'

'Very good,' said Sergeant Bird. 'Now, do you remember anything else? Did you see anybody else go out onto the terrace, for example?'

'Miss Drucker went out,' said Miss Rowland. 'She'd been wandering around, talking to people and looking tense about something. I think she was looking for someone.'

'This was after you saw her speak to Miss Dacres, yes?'

'Yes. First she followed Mr. Penk and Mr. Neale into Dorothy's room, but she came out almost immediately and went outside. She must have seen Bob on the terrace—you can ask her about that. A few minutes after that Augusta Laing and her friend went out too. Then Bob came in again, and the other three followed shortly afterwards. It wasn't long after that that all the fuss began.'

Sergeant Bird made a note. Sarah Rowland was a useful witness, for she was in a position to confirm what they had already heard from other people. It seemed that Eugene Penk and Cora Drucker had been telling the truth about their movements, which made it difficult—if not impossible—for either of them to have done it, since Penk had been on the smaller terrace during the period in question, while Cora had been in view of one person or another for the whole time.

'What about Seymour Cosgrove?' he said. 'Did you see him at all?'

'Seymour Cosgrove? He's the photographer, isn't he? I saw him earlier in the evening, looking cross. He and Augusta Laing are meant to be rather close, according to Bob, but it looked as though they'd had a quarrel, as she came to the party with someone else—Freddy, I think his name was. At one point Seymour came over to speak to her, but she stared at him down her nose and squashed him all right. Every time I saw him after that he was glowering at her or Freddy.'

'Did you see him after Miss Dacres made her announcement?'

'Not that I recall,' she replied after a moment. 'He turned up just as everybody was rushing out onto the terrace to stare down into the street, but I don't know where he was before that.'

'What about Miss Laing?'

'I don't think I saw her either,' said Sarah. 'At least, not until she went out onto the terrace with Freddy.'

'And you saw nothing that evening that gave you the slightest suspicion of what was about to happen?'

'Not at all,' she said.

It seemed that Sarah Rowland had merely succeeded in confirming that her fiancé Robert Kenrick was the most likely person to have killed Dorothy Dacres—if, indeed, anybody had done it—although there was also the question of where Augusta Laing and Seymour Cosgrove had been during the time in question. Sergeant Bird prepared to go.

'You're—you're not going to arrest him, are you?' said Sarah Rowland. Her eyes were wide and fearful. Bird took pity on her.

'Quite frankly, there's nothing we could possibly pin on him at the moment,' he said. 'We don't know how Dorothy Dacres met her death, and even if we were certain it was murder, we couldn't arrest him on the strength of what little we have.'

'He didn't do it,' she said.

'I hope for your sake you're right,' was all he said, and took his leave.

Chapter Thirteen

FOR THE NEXT few days, Freddy was kept busy covering a story about a scandalous society divorce, and had little time to think about Dorothy Dacres. On Thursday evening, however, he had just arrived home when the telephone rang. It was Gussie.

'How are you fixed for this evening?' she said. 'A bunch of us are going to the Maypole, as it's Basil and Birdie's last night at the Starlight Follies. Why don't you come along? One can always rely on the Kibbles for fireworks, so it ought to be a decent night. You can pick me up at nine if you like.'

Freddy readily accepted the invitation. He strongly suspected that Gussie's interest in him was due mainly to his press connections, but he had no objection to getting exclusive stories in this fashion—besides, she was good company, and certainly pleasing to the eye, and so he was happy enough to go along with whatever she suggested.

They arrived at the Maypole at around ten and were shown to their table, where the rest of the party were already waiting.

Freddy recognized Kenneth and Patience Neale, as well as Robert Kenrick and Sarah Rowland—who had made it up, it seemed, to judge by the sentimental glances that passed between them at frequent intervals.

'Have you heard anything more about Dorothy?' said Gussie, once they were fairly seated and the cocktails had been served.

'Ah yes, you're press, aren't you?' said Patience, who was sitting next to Gussie. 'I do hope you don't come from one of the lower publications. Some of the stories that have emerged since that dreadful night have been quite outrageous.'

Freddy could not in all honesty deny the first charge, since he worked for the *Clarion*, but he could truthfully say for once that all his pieces about Dorothy Dacres' death had been perfectly inoffensive, in conformity with Sir Aldridge Featherstone's instructions on the matter.

'I note that one paper in particular seems to have a bee in its bonnet about drugs,' she went on. 'We had a visit from a most extraordinary young man in a very loud suit, who button-holed me and my daughter outside our front door, and suggested that the doll she happened to be carrying with her at the time would be the perfect receptacle in which to smuggle "dope," as he called it. Naturally I sent him about his business immediately, but then I had to spend the morning answering awkward questions from Ada about what he meant.'

'I think I know the chap you mean,' said Freddy. 'He works for the *Herald*. He's a sad case, and to be pitied rather than blamed.'

'Oh?' said Patience.

'Yes. He's the nephew of the paper's owner. His mother was the wayward, ungovernable type, and ran away from home to join the circus as a young girl. If she'd proved tractable the family would have welcomed her back and said no more about it, but she wouldn't hear of returning home, as she'd taken up with the lion tamer and was making a modest living by putting her head into a lion's mouth twice a day. The lion tamer died tragically when he accidentally locked himself in the lion's cage at feeding time while wearing a zebra-striped fur hat, and after a suitable period of mourning she then married the elephant trainer. Things went well for a year or two, and the lady and her husband were looking forward to a happy event, when she went into the elephants' enclosure one day and rattled the gate too loudly. The oldest bull elephant—a great big bad-tempered beast—got a terrible fright, thought she was attacking him, and turned on her.'

'Goodness!' exclaimed Patience. 'What happened?'

'Oh, she was all right in the end,' said Freddy. 'There aren't many people who can claim to have survived being sat on by an elephant, but Corky's mother was one of them. Unfortunately, Corky himself didn't fare quite so well. He was born with a terrible dent in his head, and as he grew older they found that he was unable to speak anything other than complete gibberish or write any word of more than two syllables. His mother gave him up in desperation when he was four, and his uncle and aunt took him in out of pity, and eventually gave him a job at the *Herald*, where his handicap would never be noticed.'

Patience exclaimed, then the band struck up and Gussie took advantage of the noise to lean closer to Freddy and murmur:

'What bilge you do talk. You haven't changed one bit, have you?'

'I have no idea what you mean,' said Freddy blandly.

She laughed, and ordered another cocktail.

'I'm of a mind to have fun tonight,' she said. 'We've had too much misery lately, and I can't go on forever pretending to be devastated about last week.'

'Any news about the film?' said Freddy.

'No. I expect it will be put back again. It's not as though they can simply fling me in as a replacement and carry on as though nothing had happened, is it? But I refuse to be downcast. I *shall* play Helen Harper one day.'

'That's the spirit,' said Freddy. He wanted to ask Gussie where she had disappeared to after Dorothy Dacres had made her announcement, but could not think of a way to introduce the subject without causing unpleasantness. Indeed, looking about him, he could not see anyone who seemed to be upset about Dorothy, for as a result of her death a number of people were now rid of an inconvenient obstacle. Kenneth Neale would not be forced to work with an actress he had not wanted in his film, while his wife need no longer worry that her daughter would be made unhappy by cruel remarks. Gussie had been given a second chance to win the rôle that was so important to her, while Robert Kenrick was free to marry his fiancée without hindrance or interference from a woman who had been nothing but a bother to him. And what about Seymour Cosgrove? Had he been pleased at Dorothy's death? After all, she had cost him his job. How much of a grudge did he bear her? Enough to have resorted to murder?

Just as this thought passed through Freddy's head, Seymour Cosgrove himself arrived. He had evidently been invited to be one of the party, for he headed straight for their table and was greeted with enthusiasm by all except Gussie, who stiffened slightly and acknowledged him coolly. He in turn addressed her with a few words and nodded unsmilingly at Freddy. It looked as though the atmosphere were about to turn uncomfortable, but fortunately Basil and Birdie came on just then and began their act, to great applause from the crowd, and the attention of the party was necessarily occupied with them for the next twenty minutes or so. After that a troupe of dancers came on, and the Kibbles came to sit with the party. Basil sat by Freddy and fell easily into conversation with him. This was to be their last night in the show, he said. They were waiting to find out whether the production of *For Every Yesterday* was to go ahead. If not, then they had the offer of a long engagement at another night-club starting from January, but in the meantime, it would do them no harm to take a little holiday, since they had worked hard for the last few years, and Basil could not remember when they had last taken more than a day off.

While they were talking, Gussie had seen a couple she knew at another table, and she went to talk to them. Freddy looked across to see who they were, but his attention was just then arrested by the unwelcome sight of Corky Beckwith, who was sitting at a table by himself, wearing a dinner-jacket that was too short in the sleeves. Freddy got up and went across to him.

'What are you doing here?' he said without preamble.

Corky beamed at him with every appearance of pleasure.

'Freddy, old chap!' he said. 'We do seem to keep bumping into one another, don't we? How are you enjoying the cabaret? I think it's rather good. It puts me quite in mind of a little show I saw in Paris a year or two ago. Naturally, the French are much more grown-up and sensible about these things than we are, and don't require their female performers to wear clothes, or any of that nonsense. No, indeed.' He paused in happy reminiscence. 'Anyway,' he went on, 'as you can see, I'm here to enjoy the show.'

'Don't be ridiculous,' said Freddy. 'Of course you're not here to enjoy the show. You're here to spy on us—that's it, isn't it?'

'Freddy, Freddy,' said Corky. 'I am hurt, nay, distressed, that you should suspect such a thing of me. Have I not the right to disport myself in London's palaces of public entertainment just as you have? Do I not toil as arduously as the next man? Might I not pass my few hours of leisure in seeking such small enjoyment as our city affords?'

'I don't know what you think you're going to find out,' said Freddy, ignoring this. 'There's nothing funny going on.'

'Then you have nothing to worry about,' said Corky. 'I am an honest man, and seek only to unearth and conquer malfeasance and wickedness wherever it may lurk.'

'Well, there's nothing of that sort here, as you can see, so why must you keep hanging around?'

'Because it annoys you,' said Corky simply, then, as Freddy glared at him, went on: 'If you'd only done as I asked and given me an "in" with these people, then I shouldn't need to do it.'

'But you're a blister and a pestilence,' said Freddy. 'And even supposing you weren't—even supposing you were virtue and goodness personified, kind to your ageing mother and gener-ous to friends in need—nothing on this earth would induce me to admit an acquaintance with someone who is prepared to go out in public in that quite frankly horrific jacket.'

Corky merely displayed his teeth and gestured for a waiter.

'I suggest you go back to your girl-friend,' he said. 'She looks as though she needs attention. It won't do to keep a lady waiting, now, will it?'

Freddy saw that Gussie had returned to her seat and was looking across at him curiously, and went to join her.

'Isn't that that horrid journalist?' she said as he sat down again. 'Is he a friend of yours?'

'Certainly not,' said Freddy truthfully. 'He's here chasing a story, I'm afraid. He thinks one of you is dealing in cocaine.'

'Does he?' said Gussie, regarding Corky with interest. 'Which of us is it?'

'He doesn't know, but he hopes that if he follows you all about for long enough, then he'll find out.'

'I see,' said Gussie. She paused for a second. 'Do you really think Dorothy was killed deliberately? I should never have thought her the type to get mixed up with all that sort of thing, but the newspapers have been hinting that either she took the stuff and fell off the balcony while she was high, or she was murdered because of what she knew.'

'It doesn't convince you?' said Freddy.

'Not especially,' she replied. 'Somehow I can't imagine Dorothy taking dope. She was far too much the calculating type, and not at all inclined to get herself into something she couldn't get out of. I can't see her risking her career for something of that sort. Anyway, let's forget all that. I don't know anything about the cocaine, so if your friend wants a story then he'll have to make do with the one about Augusta Laing drinking far too much on a Thursday night. Will you have another?'

Never one to refuse an opportunity to make merry, Freddy readily acceded, and the next hour was spent most agreeably in the company of his new friends. True, he was permanently conscious that Corky Beckwith was watching them all through narrowed eyes, and was only looking for an opportunity to create any sort of scandal he could. And Seymour Cosgrove, too, was something of a dampener to his enjoyment, as he downed several glasses of whisky in quick succession and glowered across the table at the two of them. However, Gussie was evidently determined that nothing should spoil her fun, and encouraged Freddy enthusiastically to match her drink for drink. Soon the dancing began, and she took his hand and dragged him onto the floor. Freddy's thoughts were a little indistinct by this time, but he was aware of a certain purpose in Gussie's conduct towards him—and his suspicions were confirmed after the dance finished, and he found himself unaccountably standing in a dim corner of the room with his arms around her. He had no idea how they had got there, but it had not been his own doing, he was quite convinced of it.

'Do you like me?' she said, gazing sweetly up at him. Her voice was slightly slurred.

'I should say so,' he replied.

'Good. Then you'd better kiss me,' she said.

Freddy was an amenable sort, and not at all the type to resist the advances of a pretty girl—one, who, moreover, seemed wholly capable of asking for what she wanted without prevaricating or skipping coyly around the subject—and so he was only too happy to oblige. It was all very pleasant for a minute or two, but then he gradually became aware that somebody was standing before them, and reluctantly disengaged in order to identify the newcomer. It was Seymour Cosgrove, who fixed them both with a glare that could have melted granite.

'What do you think you're doing?' he growled.

It was perfectly obvious what they had been doing, but Freddy sensed that this was not the moment to state facts baldly.

'Oh—ah,' he managed at last. He let go of Gussie, and saw that she was looking a little shame-faced.

'Rather disgusting on your part, don't you think, to take advantage of a girl when she's been drinking?' said Seymour. His brow was knitted in a look of concentrated fury.

'I didn't—' began Freddy.

But Seymour was not listening.

'Get out of the way, Gussie,' he said. 'I'm going to knock his teeth out.'

'What? I say, that's—' said Freddy, but got no further before Seymour swept Gussie aside, grasped him by the lapels and pushed him against the wall. 'Look here, this wasn't my idea.'

'Oh, so now you're trying to throw the blame on to her, are you?' said Seymour. 'I knew you were a contemptible blighter from the moment I first saw you, but that's beyond the pale.'

'Leave him alone!' said Gussie. 'Seymour, you're being an idiot.'

Seymour gave her a withering look.

'I thought you had better taste than to fasten onto this pathetic specimen,' he said. 'Why, I'll bet his mother still brings him breakfast in bed every morning.'

'I say,' said Freddy, stung.

'Be quiet!' said Seymour. 'Now listen, my girl. I'm taking you home this minute. I won't stand here and watch you making a fool of yourself in front of everybody.'

'But we weren't doing it in front of everybody,' Freddy pointed out, as Gussie protested. 'We picked a nice, quiet corner so as not to offend anyone.'

If this remark was intended to restore calm, it failed miserably. Seymour gave a roar, grabbed Freddy again and shook him hard.

'Ow! Get off me, won't you?' said Freddy through gritted teeth. 'It's not my fault you can't hold onto a girl without clubbing her over the head and chaining her up.'

Again, this was perhaps not the best thing to say to an already enraged Seymour Cosgrove. Freddy realized this fact as soon as he had uttered the words, and decided to make himself scarce. However, Seymour was too quick for him: as Freddy made a dash for it, Seymour launched himself at his legs and tackled him to the ground. They rolled on the floor, knocking over a chair as they did so, and causing several ladies to scream. Freddy clutched desperately at his neck and went purple as Seymour did his best to throttle him, while Gussie pulled ineffectually at Seymour's jacket in an attempt to drag him off. At last, Freddy lifted a hand and grabbed Seymour's face in desperation, squeezing it hard until he let go suddenly with a yell of pain.

'You nearly poked my eye out!' he said in outrage. 'That's cheating.' He stood up and hauled Freddy to his feet. 'Let's do this properly. Fists or nothing.'

'What?' panted Freddy in disbelief. 'I'm not going to fight you.'

'Oh, yes you are,' said Seymour, and swung a punch, which connected with Freddy's jaw and almost laid him out. He fell back against a table, causing more screams, then rose unsteadily, and was testing his jaw to see whether it was broken when Seymour swung at him again. Freddy ducked just in time, and turned to run, but his way was impeded by people, so he did the only thing he could think of and dived under a table. He emerged on the other side, hoping he was safe, but Seymour was not giving up. He threw himself across the table at Freddy and brought him down again next to their party. From his position on the floor, Freddy could see the upside-down faces of Robert Kenrick and Sarah Rowland, but he had no time to register anything more than their expressions of consternation before Seymour began pummelling him hard, leaving Freddy no option but to put his arms over his face and curl up as small as he could, in order to avoid being beaten to a pulp. Fortunately for him, Seymour was too drunk to hit effectively, although he made up for his inefficiency with a great energy and devotion to his task, and so it looked as though the result might be much the same anyway if somebody did not come to the rescue soon.

'Help him!' cried Gussie.

'Now, then,' came the voice of Kenneth Neale. 'Seymour, old chap, you'd better get off.'

'The police are here,' came another voice; Freddy thought it might be that of Patience Neale.

'*What*?' said someone else.

And then stern orders were heard, and hands were laid upon Seymour Cosgrove, and he was pulled off. Freddy lay winded on the floor as people chattered excitedly all around him. It was only then that he noticed the music had stopped; he supposed idly that he and Seymour were the entertainment now. After a moment a policeman helped Freddy to his feet, and he glanced around warily, and saw that Seymour was being escorted towards the door under protest by two sturdy-looking bobbies.

'Are you all right?' said a voice next to him, and he turned to see Sarah Rowland staring at him in concern.

'I think I should like to sit down,' he said, and did so. His jaw was beginning to throb painfully, but as far as he could tell there was no blood. A little way away he saw Corky Beckwith scribbling busily in a notebook. He appeared to be in some sort of ecstatic trance. Freddy let out a small groan and closed his eyes.

'Perhaps you ought to get home, sir,' suggested the policeman.

'Aren't you arresting me?' said Freddy in surprise.

'Not this time. We have a number of witnesses who say the chap attacked you. He'll be spending tonight in the cells, and if you want to bring an action against him, you'll have plenty of evidence.'

'No, no, I don't think I do,' said Freddy weakly.

Once they had ascertained to their satisfaction that order had been restored, the police departed, and the waiters were left to clear up the mess. The band struck up again, and soon it was as though the fight had never happened. Freddy sat, attempting feebly to brush himself down, but then gave it up. Robert Kenrick pressed a glass of whisky upon him, and he took a gulp and felt a little better. Then someone sat down next to him. It was Gussie.

'I need to talk to you,' she said in a low, urgent voice.

'You're not going to kiss me again, are you?' he said in sudden fear.

'Don't be silly, it's nothing to do with that,' she said impatiently. Her manner had changed completely, and she looked worried. 'Listen, you may as well take me home, then I can tell you about it on the way.'

Freddy was too tired to make any objection, and so a few minutes later they left.

'What is it?' he said, once they were out in the street.

She looked about her to make sure there was nobody nearby, then dug in her little tasselled bag and handed him something. It was a folded paper packet.

'I found this in my handbag,' she said.

Freddy unwrapped it carefully, although he already knew what he would find inside it.

'Cocaine?' he said, regarding the white powder.

'I assume that's what it is,' she said. 'But it's nothing to do with me.'

'Then how did it get into your bag?'

'I don't know, but I'd very much like to find out. If I didn't know better, I'd say someone was trying to get me into trouble.' Freddy looked at her, and she went on, 'I was looking for a handkerchief to give you after the police arrived, and found it then. You'll think me silly, but after what you said about that reporter, my first thought was that this whole thing was a deliberate trap, and so I shoved it down the back of the seat cushion just in case the police decided to search everybody. Then when they'd gone I thought I'd better show you, so I got it back.'

'When did you last look in your bag?' said Freddy.

'When Basil and Birdie were on, I think. I couldn't remember whether I had my lipstick with me or not.'

'And you're sure the dope wasn't there then?'

'No,' she said. 'I mean, yes, I'm sure. I don't carry much in it, so I'd have noticed straightaway.'

'But why would somebody plant it on you?' said Freddy. 'Do you have any enemies?'

'Not that I know of. I mean to say, I'm sure there must be people who dislike me, but I don't think anybody hates me enough to do something like that. And besides, everyone who was there tonight is my friend.'

Freddy said nothing for a moment. He was remembering the look on Corky Beckwith's face as he scribbled in his notebook, and an awful suspicion was beginning to dawn. Corky had been at the Maypole tonight, and Gussie had found a mysterious packet of cocaine in her bag. He had also been at the

Abingdon on the night Dorothy died—and a quantity of the drug had been found there, too. Freddy could not help thinking back to the night of Dorothy's death, when he had discovered Corky scrabbling around in Cora Drucker's dressing-table. Corky had claimed he was looking for cocaine, but was that really the case? Had he, in fact, been looking for an opportunity to *plant* it? There was no denying he had an *idée fixe* about the stuff—as did his paper, the *Herald*. Corky was certainly unprincipled enough to do something of the kind, even if he had never been caught at it before. And Dorothy's friends had all seemed very surprised at the news that cocaine had been found among her belongings; they had had no idea that she took it, they said. Was the whole drugs angle a red herring, then? Did it have anything to do with Dorothy's death at all?

Just then Freddy was struck by an even worse thought. Was it possible—might Corky have—but no; it was unthinkable! Corky was the most unscrupulous of men, but surely even he would not stoop to murder purely for the purposes of getting a story. And yet, now the idea was in his head, Freddy could not quite let go of it. He thought back to that fatal evening, racking his brain to try and remember what Corky had been doing during the period between Freddy's catching him in Cora's room and Dorothy's death. Had he somehow managed to sneak out onto the terrace, creep up on Dorothy unawares and shove her over the edge? It did not seem likely. And yet— and yet it was such a beautiful solution to the mystery, if it were true.

One thing was certain: it was absolutely necessary that someone keep a close eye on Corky for the next few days. If he really was planting drugs all over London, then he ought to be stopped, before someone was unjustly arrested, or worse. It was late now, but Freddy resolved that tomorrow he should think of some plan to keep Corky in sight. For now, his jaw was aching and all he wanted to do was to collapse into bed and sleep for twelve hours, and so he took his leave of Gussie as quickly as he decently could and went home.

Chapter Fourteen

CORKY MUST SOMEHOW have managed to get his copy in before the *Herald* went to bed, for the next morning the paper ran a story about the fight at the Maypole, which dwelt with great and malicious glee on the bad behaviour of the upper classes, and those in the film business who thought they could do as they liked without fear of consequences. Meanwhile Freddy, much to his disgust, was given a carpeting by his editor, Mr. Bickerstaffe, for bringing the *Clarion* into disrepute. In vain did he try to explain that the fracas had not been his fault, and that he had been attacked. His protestations did no good at all, for his red eyes and the swelling bruise on his jaw did not exactly speak of an evening virtuously spent—and indeed, he could hardly confess what had provoked Seymour's attack on him without looking like the worst sort of bounder, for it did not do to make a public exhibition of oneself with another man's girl, even if the couple were currently not on good terms. So he put his head down and muttered an apology, and was at last allowed to go back to his desk, where Jolliffe regarded him with sympathy and something like envy.

'Fighting again, old chap?' he said. 'I don't know how you get into these messes.'

'Nor do I,' said Freddy bitterly, feeling his jaw with care, for he was still not entirely sure it was not broken.

'I must say, your life is much more interesting than mine,' said Jolliffe. 'I had a very quiet evening at the picture palace. They were showing one of Dorothy Dacres' old films—as a sort of tribute, I think. All silent, of course. The new one was to be a talkie.'

'*Was* to be a talkie?' said Freddy.

'Well, *is*, I suppose. But I don't know when they're going to start. It's a dreadfully complicated business, you know. They don't just grab any old person off the street and point a camera at them. That's how they used to do it, but these days there are all sorts of things they have to consider. There's a lot of money tied up in it now. It's quite possible they might decide to start the whole process again, with a completely new script and cast.'

'I see,' said Freddy, thinking of Gussie.

Jolliffe went away shortly afterwards, and Freddy was left to his own reflections. His head was aching and he had little inclination to work, but he was feeling resentful after the carpeting he had received, and whether Corky were a murderer, an *agent provocateur*, or merely the most irritating man in London, Freddy was determined to get one up on him one way or another. But how to do it? Freddy's chief concern was to discover whether Corky had, in fact, been planting drugs on innocent people in order to obtain copy. He might easily have done it at both the Abingdon and the Maypole. If he had, then presumably he had intended to call the police anonymously on both occasions and have them conduct a search. The first time he had been forestalled in his plan by the death of Dorothy Dacres; and there had been no need for him to call the police last night either, for the brawl had seen to that. The only flaw in Freddy's theory there was that the police had not searched anybody at the Maypole, but had merely arrested Seymour and left, whereas surely Corky's intention had been for Gussie to be caught with the cocaine. Perhaps everything had happened too fast, and events had overtaken him, leaving him no opportunity to point the finger at her.

After ruminating for a while, Freddy realized that he would not achieve anything by moping in the office, and went out. The *Herald* building was just along the street, and Freddy hovered outside it for a few minutes. It was raining, however, and he was hardly feeling his best, so in the end he went and sat in the window of a tea-shop across the way. After three cups of strong coffee and a cream scone, he was feeling better, and was just wondering whether to order a second scone when he saw Corky Beckwith himself coming out of the *Herald*'s offices. Quickly, Freddy threw down a few coins and left the tea-shop. Corky was walking briskly along the other side of the street, heading East towards St. Paul's, and Freddy followed him at a discreet distance, wondering where he was going. At length, Corky turned left into Fetter Lane and Freddy hurried across the road after him, taking care not to be seen—although he need not have worried, for Corky seemed to have no suspicion he was being followed. Was he on the trail of the drugs gang, Freddy wondered.

Soon they arrived at Holborn Circus, and Corky stopped for a moment, looking about him. Freddy ducked into a doorway and waited. Then Corky was on the move again. He dived across Holborn, catching Freddy by surprise, and in through the door of Gamages. Freddy sighed as he noticed the unusually large number of people milling in and out of the shop, and saw the gaudy signs in the window, announcing the first day of the Christmas Bazaar. After a moment's thought he followed Corky through the door. Perhaps he had come to buy something and would soon be on his way. But no; after fighting his way through the throng, Freddy eventually spotted the familiar tall figure, standing in among a crowd of excited children, looking at a display of model trains as they whizzed in and out of tunnels. He wore a camera around his neck, but seemed to have forgotten all about it as he gazed in a sort of rapture at the display, hands clasped together. Freddy rolled his eyes impatiently. A children's toy fair was not what he had expected, but it looked as though this was what his quarry had come for—and sure enough, after a few minutes, Corky came to himself and began fiddling with his camera. He was shortly afterwards approached by a very dignified personage who appeared to belong to the store, and the two entered into conversation. Corky seemed to be explaining his purpose there, and evidently he passed muster, for the dignified personage immediately began to pick out the cleanest and most likely-looking children for a photograph. This process took some little time, but was eventually concluded to everyone's satisfaction. By now, Freddy was convinced that he would find out nothing today, and was on the point of leaving, when Corky happened to glance up and spot him.

'Hallo!' he said cheerfully. 'Have you come to see the trains too? Simply marvellous, aren't they?' Gone was his usual patronizing manner, and he seemed genuinely enthusiastic. 'I always make sure they send me to cover the opening of the Bazaar. I find it quite thrilling—just like being a child all over again!'

A number of possible remarks sprang to Freddy's lips, but he held them in, for he had suddenly had an idea.

'Yes, I suppose it's all very nice,' he said. 'Have you finished here? I want to talk to you.'

'I think so,' said Corky. 'Let me speak to this chap again, then I'll see you outside in five minutes if you like.'

Freddy nodded and fought his way through the sea of children until he reached the street again. Corky joined him shortly afterwards.

'What is it?' he said. 'I hope you're not going to be bothersome about that little piece this morning. You could hardly expect me not to print it. Why, you practically handed it to me on a plate!'

'No,' said Freddy. 'At least, not exactly. Do you remember what you said the other day about a *quid pro quo*?'

'Ye-es,' said Corky, eyeing him speculatively.

'Well, what about it?'

'What have you got? And why are you so amenable all of a sudden?'

Freddy swallowed and prepared to lay it on with a trowel.

'I dare say you won't care two hoots about it,' he said, 'but I got a good wigging this morning from old Bickerstaffe about that "little piece," as you call it. He as good as threatened me with the boot if I didn't start toeing the line. It all got rather unpleasant, and now I need to come up with something pretty nifty—and soon, or I'll be out of a job.'

'I see,' said Corky. 'Does that mean you're prepared to help me with this dope story? Do you know something, perchance? Has one of your friends mortgaged his title and blued his inheritance on a trunkful of happy dust?'

Freddy made a show of reluctance.

'I can't tell you at the moment,' he said unwillingly. 'Let's just say I've heard something in the past few days that caused me to think carefully about what you said. Someone I know dropped something that caught me completely by surprise, because he's not at all the sort to get himself mixed up in this kind of thing. Now, there's no use in your asking me any more about it just yet, because I know perfectly well he won't talk at present—in fact, he didn't intend to tell me about it at all, but it slipped out when he'd had a few drinks. However, I'm due to go down to his family pile and stay with them in a week or two—it's a yearly thing, you know—and I hope I shall be able to get him to say more about it then. I want to convince him to give the stuff up, and to give me the name of the person who's been supplying it to him, but in the meantime, I thought you and I might work together on your end of the story.'

Corky was listening attentively.

'This *friend* of yours,' he said. 'Is there any connection between him and the Dacres crowd?'

Freddy hesitated.

'Only a slight one—but enough to make it more than likely that the supplier is the same one in both cases,' he said.

'Hmm,' said Corky. 'I should like to know the name of this person to whom you refer.'

'I told you, I won't say,' said Freddy. 'I'll never betray a pal— and besides, he's not the one we're after, is he? Unless you were telling fibs when you said you were looking for the supplier. Heaven forbid you were just looking for some society names to print in that rag of yours.'

'Heaven forbid!' agreed Corky. 'No, you're right—it is the supplier I want. But I shouldn't bank too heavily on your friend's coming through this unscathed, you know. Once we catch the fellow, I dare say all sorts of names will come out into the open.'

'Not his name,' said Freddy. 'He's been using a false one, you see. I think he'll be safe.'

Corky directed an odd look at him, and seemed to be think-ing. At last he came to a decision.

'Very well,' he said. 'I accept your request to form a tempo-rary partnership. It's obvious you haven't told me the whole story, but I rather think I've guessed the most important facts.' Here he winked knowingly. 'Still, the secret is safe with me— just so long as you play the game and don't try and double-cross me. If you do, then I warn you: it's every man for himself.'

'Oh, certainly,' said Freddy humbly. 'I shouldn't expect any-thing else.'

'Very well,' said Corky. 'Then we're agreed. Now, I suppose you'd like to hear about all the hard work I've been doing while you've been out living the high life every night. I've been waiting for the past few weeks to hear from an informant of mine who occasionally passes me useful information from his friends in the East End. He was under orders to communicate with me if he received news of a particular cargo having arrived safely at Tilbury without being intercepted at Customs. They've been on the alert lately, and have caught a good few consignments, so things have been quiet on that score in recent times. However, I finally had the signal from my chap this morning that something was about to happen, and so I propose we go along and keep a look-out.'

'Do you mean the stuff has made it as far as London?' said Freddy.

'Yes, I think so—or it's about to. There's a concern just off Commercial Street that I occasionally make it my business to walk past, having had certain hints with regard to its real purpose, although I haven't come up with much up to now— most likely because it's always been the wrong time. However, now that we know for sure there's been a consignment, I think it's safe to say that something is going to happen, and soon.'

'They're going to divvy the stuff up and dole it out, you mean?'

'Yes. They can't keep it too long, you see. They need to pass it on as quickly as possible, so they're never caught with the goods.'

'What do you intend to do, then?'

'Well, I don't expect much to happen before this evening. The stuff comes to Whitechapel via a circuitous route—Epping and Barnet, and places like that—so as not to attract attention. But I think if we watch the house this evening we might find out something interesting.'

'You mean the delivery boys will come and collect their shares?' said Freddy.

'Exactly.'

'But how shall we find out who we're looking for? I mean to say, there must be lots of these types. How will we know which one to follow?'

Corky tapped his nose confidentially.

'My chap's a wary one,' he said, 'and didn't want to give anything more than the vaguest information. The only reason he told me anything at all is that he needs money for his own habit, and the *Herald* pays generously. I've had to work hard to persuade him that I'm not about to blow the gaff to the police— at least, not at his end. But I got the information out of him all right. I said we needed to know which of the suppliers worked the West End, and the top-notch clubs in particular. It's not the middle-men we're interested in, I told him—it's the people in high society who take the stuff when they ought to be setting an example to the rest of us.'

'You told him a pack of lies, you mean?'

'Of course not. It was all perfectly true. What interest have I in shutting down their business? Why, I'd find myself with nothing to write about.'

'Spoken like a true reporter,' said Freddy ironically.

'At any rate, he gave me a description of the man we want. All we have to do is lie in wait for him and follow him to see where he goes.'

'Look here,' said Freddy. 'Is this all on the level?'

'It had better be,' replied Corky. 'I've had to pay the man rather a lot of money. So, then, what do you say we meet at six or so, have something to eat to fortify ourselves for the long night ahead, and then get down to business?'

Freddy hesitated, but agreed, and the two men parted ways until that evening. Freddy stood, apparently gazing at the display in the shop window, although in reality he was deep in thought. He had not seriously believed Corky's story about the drugs, since it seemed too convenient for words, and he had proposed joining forces with his rival on the spur of the moment, with a view to keeping him close and perhaps inducing him to confess that he had been responsible for planting the cocaine in Dorothy Dacres' hotel room and Gussie's handbag. But now it appeared that Corky really did believe the Dacres case was connected to a drugs ring. Had Freddy got it all wrong, then? His instinct for these things was usually good, and he had been almost sure that the cocaine was merely a red herring, and that Dorothy had been killed for quite different reasons. But what if Corky were right? It was a ghastly idea, but Freddy was forced to admit it was a possibility.

He turned away from the window, and headed back towards Fleet Street. He did not much relish the idea of spending the evening with Corky Beckwith, but perhaps their little outing would shed some light on the subject.

Chapter Fifteen

THE RAIN HAD stopped and a stiff, cold breeze had got up by the time Freddy and Corky arrived at Aldgate. Freddy was in a particularly grumpy mood, for he had the awful feeling that the night was going to end in trouble, and that he ought not to have agreed to this, since Corky's methods were of the sort to raise eyebrows in any right-thinking person, and even Freddy had his standards. Still, if he wanted to find out whether Corky had been interfering in the Dacres case, there was no choice but to go along with him. So it was that at half past seven they found themselves standing in the shadow of a doorway across the street from a run-down haberdasher's shop, which plied its trade on a narrow turn-off from Commercial Street.

'This is the place, you see,' said Corky. 'Looks perfectly above the board, doesn't it? Come here during the day and you'll find it operates as a quite legitimate business—or appears to, at any rate. You'll see respectable housewives coming in and out at all times of day, ostensibly buying thread and lace trimming and suchlike—but let me tell you, those women are not what they seem. They're the wives—if they even bother to call themselves that—of some of the worst degenerates in London. These low types send their womenfolk in to receive instructions as to when they are to come in and collect the stuff. It's all given in code, of course. You know the sort of thing: two yards of white twill means "come tonight," while a bobbin of red cotton means "stay clear."'

'I see,' said Freddy, looking at the shop with interest.

'I expect if we'd come here earlier, we'd have seen they were having a particularly busy day,' said Corky. 'Word will have got around that the shipment's come in, you see.'

There was nothing to show the place was anything out of the ordinary. At the front was the door to the shop, and from where they were standing they could see a little passage running down the side of the building, quite in the shadows.

'There's a door down there,' said Corky. 'Our lot will come and go that way, I should think.'

'I take it we wait, then,' said Freddy.

Corky nodded. They stood in the darkness in silence for some time. Freddy was cold, for the wind was keen. He wished he had worn a thicker coat and had thought to bring a scarf. He was beginning to feel stiff, so he shifted his position and was about to say something when Corky held up a hand and said, 'Shh!'

Someone was approaching along the quiet street. It was a man. His cap was pulled low over his face, and his hands were deep in his pockets. He was looking neither right nor left. As he reached the haberdasher's shop, he dived suddenly down the passage.

'That's the first,' whispered Corky.

'Is it our man?' said Freddy.

Corky shook his head and put a finger over his lips. They watched. After a few minutes, the man emerged again and set off back the way he had come. Then another man came. He, too, was in and out in a very few minutes. Then two men came at once, from different directions. Over the next hour more men came, and some women too. Some looked furtive, others strode confidently and whistled cheerfully as though to allay suspicion, while still others walked halfway past the shop, then seemed to remember something and turned back and knocked on the door.

'Hear that knock?' said Corky. 'Four then two, otherwise nobody will answer.'

They waited some time longer, but nobody else came. Freddy was beginning to get impatient. It seemed indeed as though there were some story here, but it was not the one he had been looking for. He was about to suggest they go to the police and hand the information to them—although he knew Corky would be unwilling—when Corky again held his hand up.

'This is the one,' he whispered.

Freddy had been so deep in thought that he had not noticed the approach of another newcomer. This one was very different from the others, who had been ill-favoured specimens to a man, for he was clean and spruce, and dressed in a suit, and looked more like a solicitor's clerk than anything else. He walked down the street with a light, quick step, knocked on the door smartly as though he had no objection to being seen or heard, and disappeared inside the shop. After a few minutes he reappeared and set off in the direction of the Underground station, unaware that he was being followed by Freddy and Corky. He leapt onto a train heading West, as did his pursuers, but alighted soon after, at Charing Cross, and headed towards Covent Garden. He was walking fast, which made it difficult to follow him, but after a minute or two he slowed down and took more of an interest in his surroundings. He stopped outside one or two eating establishments to examine the bill of fare, and seemed to be considering whether to go into one of them. Instead, he glanced at his watch and carried on, his pursuers still behind him.

At length he turned into Wellington Street and paused outside the theatre there to read a playbill. The evening's performance had just ended, and the theatre was disgorging its patrons onto the pavement outside. The crowd was a distraction, and made it difficult for Freddy and Corky to keep their quarry in sight. For a moment he disappeared from view, but then Freddy spotted him trying to push his way through the crowd, and hastened after him. Alas! Just then a stern-looking gentleman bellowed an instruction, and the crowd parted, with the assistance of one or two public-spirited young men, who held out their arms as a sort of barrier, to allow an elderly lady with two walking-sticks to pass out to a waiting motor-car. Freddy and Corky fidgeted in great agitation—indeed, there is no saying that Corky might not have pushed the old woman out of the way had he been near enough to do it—

then threaded their way through the crowd to the other side, but it was too late; the man had gone. In vain did they search down the side streets, and peer in through the windows of the restaurants and the public-houses; their quarry had completely vanished. Had he perhaps known they were following him, and taken steps to shake them off?

At last they were forced to give up the search, for it was obvious that he had got the better of them, and they returned to stand across the street from the theatre and curse their misfortune.

'It's too bad,' grumbled Corky, who was particularly vexed that he had come so close to getting the story of a lifetime, only to see it snatched from beneath his nose. 'Who knows when the next delivery will come in? It might be weeks before they manage to smuggle any more into London. And I shall have to pay my informant all over again, which won't go down at all well with the powers that be at the paper. They won't be any too pleased that I lost my chance.'

Freddy, who was more upset at having spent so long waiting in the cold for nothing, and was uninterested in the matter of Corky's expenses, shrugged.

'There's still the story of the Commercial Street shop,' he said. 'The police will certainly like to hear about that. Why don't we telephone the Yard? That way at least we haven't wasted an entire evening.'

'What? And miss the really big story?' said Corky. 'Are you quite mad? If we go and tell the police about the shop, then they'll close it down and arrest the owners, and I'll get a small paragraph on page twenty that nobody will read. Then the supplies will begin coming in from somewhere else and going to a different house, and I'll be back where I started, and all my hard work will have been for nothing. No, I won't have it, I tell you. I've spent weeks on this story, and I know it will be a big one if only I can find out the name of the final link in the chain.'

'Well, it's all off for this evening, at any rate,' said Freddy. 'You'll just have to wait until you hear from your man again. In the meantime, I think I shall go home. Goodnight.'

He turned to leave, but just then his attention was caught by a figure which emerged from Exeter Street, hat pulled low onto its head, and headed towards the theatre as though in a great hurry. Corky saw the newcomer at the same time and stiffened, and both men backed quietly into the shadows on their side of the road, so as not to be spotted. A few late stragglers were still emerging from the theatre, and on seeing them the figure slowed to a casual stroll, then paused by the portico, apparently to search in its pockets for a handkerchief. As the last theatre-goer passed, the figure glanced about, then darted across to the main door, which was flanked by two large plant-pots containing ornamental trees. It stopped for a second, and seemed to peer into one of the pots. Then, as quickly as it had arrived, it hurried off again. Of one accord, Freddy and Corky emerged from the shadows and set off in pursuit of the figure, which was heading with rapid steps in the direction of Charing Cross. Their quarry seemed to have no suspicion that anyone was following, and once at a safe distance from the theatre, paused by a street-lamp to light a cigarette and glance briefly around again. That one glance was enough to make it certain, for the yellow light from above threw his features into sharp relief, revealing a familiar face. Corky and Freddy exchanged looks.

'Well, well,' murmured Corky. 'Basil Kibble, as I live and breathe!'

CHAPTER SIXTEEN

WHEN THEY ARRIVED at Charing Cross, Freddy and Corky hung back and watched as Basil Kibble bought a ticket for Kennington, then followed him down to the platform and stood well away from him until the train arrived. The journey was a short one, and when they reached Kennington, Basil hurried out of the station and into a warren of deserted streets. It was so quiet that Freddy and Corky had to take great care not to be seen or heard, but they followed him as silently as they could as he turned right, then left, then right again. At last he turned into a street of modest terraced houses, and ran up the steps of the second house along and in through the front door. Fearful of being seen, and anxious to shelter from the wind, Freddy and Corky retired to a shadowy spot against a garden wall around the corner.

'This must be where they live,' said Freddy. 'Now what? We don't absolutely know that he picked anything up.'

'It can't be a coincidence,' said Corky. 'Our man passes the theatre, deposits his package under cover of the crowd, and

Kibble picks it up as soon as the coast is clear. That's where the supplier must have gone when we lost him: he met Kibble and took the payment, and told him where to find the stuff. That way, if anybody tried to arrest them while the money was being handed over they'd find no drugs on either of them.'

'We still don't have proof, though,' said Freddy. 'All we have is two people passing the same spot within ten minutes of one another.'

'Yes, so we'd better go and see what Basil and Birdie are up to. There's no doubt they're both in it up to the eyes. What do you say to a little peek through the area window?'

'I suppose there's no way of getting into the back?' said Freddy. He turned and looked behind him at the wall against which they were standing. It was about seven feet high, and had a wooden door set into it. 'See here—this door must lead into the back yard of the end house. The Kibbles are in the second house along. If we could get in through here and then climb across the fence into their yard, we'd be less visible.'

Corky tried the door, but it was locked.

'No good,' he said. 'We might get over the wall if you gave me a leg-up, but I shouldn't like to risk it—look.' He indicated the window of a house opposite, from which a dim light glowed. 'There's too much danger of our being seen.'

'All right, then, let's try the area, as you suggest,' said Freddy. He had quite forgotten his desire to go home, and was now determined to see the adventure through to the end.

They returned to the Kibbles' street. Here, there were no lights burning inconveniently in nearby houses, but there *was* a light coming from the area window of the Kibbles' house. The curtains were not fully drawn, so they would have to be very careful not to be seen or heard. Freddy put his hand on the wrought-iron gate at the top of the steps, but Corky nudged him and shook his head. He glanced around and brought something out of his pocket. It was a little bottle.

'Brilliantine,' he whispered. 'In case the gate squeaks.'

'Is this something you do often?' said Freddy.

'It's always as well to be prepared,' said Corky. He took out a handkerchief and with great efficiency proceeded to oil the gate. It opened without a sound, and they crept down the steps and stood each to one side of the window. Corky leaned cautiously across to peer through the chink in the curtains. After a minute, Freddy joined him. Through the gap he had a glimpse of a bare floor and walls, and one or two shabby bits of furniture. A lamp on the far wall gave off a dull, pink light, casting a dim glow over everything. In the middle of the room was a low coffee-table which was missing a leg, and was propped up by a packing-case. On the table was a bottle of whisky that was almost empty, a glass, and a small paper parcel which looked as though it might easily have been carried in a pocket. Was this what Basil had collected from the plant pot outside the theatre?

The biggest piece of furniture in the room was a sofa, on which Birdie Kibble was currently reclining, fully dressed and seemingly fast asleep. Her mouth was open and one arm dangled over the edge of the cushion towards the floor. As they watched, Basil came in and regarded her with a look of disgust. He lifted her hand and let it drop, then bent over her and slapped her cheek sharply several times, but she made no move. He straightened up again and glanced at the parcel on the table. He picked it up and looked around, as though seeking a better place to put it. At last he shoved it under the sofa and left the room. Freddy and Corky watched for a few minutes more, but Birdie remained motionless and recumbent. Nothing else happened, except that a light went on on the top floor. A few minutes later it went out again, and the watchers returned to their place by the wall around the corner to discuss what to do next. The light in the opposite window had gone out, and all was quiet, apart from the rustling of dry leaves in the wind.

'*Now* may we go to the police?' said Freddy.

'No,' said Corky. 'They won't listen to us without evidence.'

'They'll take our word for it, surely? Or at least, they'll investigate.'

Corky coughed.

'I may—er—be temporarily *persona non grata* with the chaps at the Yard at present,' he said. 'A minor matter of my having been a little too enthusiastic in my attempts to assist them in a recent case of burglary.'

'What happened?'

'A constable of my acquaintance happened to let slip that they were planning a raid on the gang's hide-out. I was rather keen to get a nice, colourful piece out of it, so I slipped along there myself in order not to miss anything, and in so doing accidentally alerted the thieves to the arrival of the police. Naturally, they skipped, and the raid turned into something of a damp squib.'

'Oh, I heard about that. Was that you?' said Freddy. 'Ass. They'll never catch them now. All right, then, what else do you suggest?'

'We'll need evidence if they're to believe us,' said Corky. 'And it was there on the table in front of us. We must get hold of that packet.'

'Nothing easier,' said Freddy. 'I'll just go and knock on the door and ask for it, shall I? I'm sure they'll be delighted to hand it over.'

'You do like your little joke,' said Corky. 'Of course I wasn't suggesting that.'

'Then what? You don't want to break into the place, I hope.'

'We may not have to break anything if the area door's unlocked or the window's not fastened,' said Corky.

'Of course it will be fastened. What sort of idiot doesn't lock up at night?'

'The sort who spends her evenings lying doped and unconscious on a sofa, perhaps? You saw her just then. If we do manage to get in she'll never wake up.'

'She might not, but Basil looked perfectly sober to me,' said Freddy.

'Tchah! He's gone to bed, two floors up. He won't hear a thing.'

Freddy still seemed inclined to shake his head. Corky gave a theatrical start, as though he had just realized something, then regarded Freddy with a sneering expression.

'Oh, I see,' he said. 'You're afraid! That's it, isn't it?'

'I'm not afraid,' said Freddy crossly. 'I don't want to spend the night in a police cell and then get the boot, that's all.'

'Do you mean to say the *Clarion* would sack you for such a minor transgression as that?' said Corky. 'I'd always heard they were a little on the milk-and-water side about this sort of thing, but surely not when there's a story this big at stake? Don't you see how important it is? It goes to the very heart of society! If film stars and bigwigs have been corrupted, then what hope is there for the rest of us? Why, we may as well give it all up now and abandon ourselves, unresisting, to the grasping clutches of the Devil himself!'

'What piffle you do talk,' said Freddy. 'Oh, very well, then, I suppose it can't hurt to try. Mind—if we can't get in then we must come away.'

'Naturally,' said Corky. 'And if we *are* successful and this comes off, then I might consider speaking to my editor about offering you a junior position at the *Herald*. Now, what do you say to that?'

Freddy threw him a pained look and set off back around the corner to the Kibbles' house without waiting for him. Once in the area again, they saw that Birdie had not moved an inch.

'Do you suppose she's all right?' said Freddy. 'I wonder whether we oughtn't to call a doctor. That's not cocaine she's taken, surely?'

'I don't care what she's taken,' said Corky. 'All I care is that she stays asleep long enough for us to get hold of that package.' He turned and regarded a door whose peeling paint and rusting lock indicated it had not been used for some time. 'Hmm. No go there. What about the window?'

'Locked, of course,' said Freddy.

Corky moved to examine it.

'This ought to be easy enough,' he said, feeling in his pocket. He brought out a penknife, inserted it between the two sashes and began to move it back and forth carefully. 'I'm trying to dislodge the catch,' he explained. 'Ah—there! Simple, when you know the trick.'

'I thought we weren't going to break in,' whispered Freddy, as Corky lifted the lower sash slowly, so as not to make a noise.

But Corky merely gestured for silence again. They waited, to be sure Birdie would not wake up, then Corky climbed in through the window. After a moment, Freddy followed. In a trice Corky had retrieved the package from under the sofa and was unwrapping it, barely glancing at the unconscious woman who lay there.

'This is the stuff, all right,' he whispered with glee, then wrapped it back up and put it in his pocket. 'Now, is there anything else?'

'Not that I can see,' said Freddy, who had taken in the rest of the room at a glance. It was so bare that there seemed nowhere to hide anything. 'Is there anything else under that sofa?'

Corky peered underneath.

'Nothing. Perhaps we ought to search the rest of the house,' he said.

'Look here,' said Freddy. 'We can't just stroll around the place as though we owned it. You said we'd pick up the package and then leave.'

'Yes, but—' began Corky.

Just then, there was a sound like a murmur behind them, and they both started and looked around. Birdie had shifted her position on the sofa, although she had not woken up.

'You see?' hissed Freddy. 'Now, you may stay here if you like, but I'm going. It's late and we've got the evidence we came for.

You've got everything you need for your story—and more—so there's no sense in hanging about.'

'Oh, all right,' said Corky sulkily. 'I just thought if we searched the house we might find something else of interest.'

'Well, I hardly think they have any silver to steal, if that's what you mean,' said Freddy. 'It's pretty obvious they're not exactly quids in.'

He went across to the window and prepared to swing himself up onto the sill, but before he could do so he heard an exclamation from Corky behind him, and turned just in time to see the door to the room opening. Had he been a split second quicker Freddy might have made a leap for it, but he was too late, and he froze. It was not the sight of Basil Kibble that caused him to stand stock still, but the revolver he was pointing directly at Freddy.

CHAPTER SEVENTEEN

'WHAT THE DEVIL do you think you're doing?' said Basil, without lowering the gun. He was wearing a dressing-gown and a hair-net, and the expression on his face was anything but friendly.

Corky and Freddy gazed warily at the revolver.

'Don't I know you?' said Basil suddenly, looking at Freddy.

Freddy thought quickly. He swayed slightly, and beamed with great affection at Basil.

'Yes,' he said, slurring his words a little. 'Awfully sorry to barge in on you like this, old bean, but you see, Corky here and I have been out on the town this evening—had a rather good night at Bertolino's, in fact. But Corky's never been able to hold his drink, and after a few too many martinis there was an unfortunate incident with a waitress. Purely a misunderstanding, of course, and not at all intentional, but naturally she wasn't going to put up with that sort of thing, so they asked us politely to leave the premises. Actually, now I come to think of it they weren't all *that* polite, were they?' he said, turning to Corky.

Corky hiccupped and shook his head sorrowfully.

'At any rate, the town may have wanted rid of us but we weren't quite ready to leave the town. I mean to say, I should never be able to hold my head up again at my club if I slunk back home before four on a Friday night. But Corky has one of those faces that seem to rub doormen up the wrong way. I don't know what it is, but as soon as they catch sight of him their first instinct is to shy in horror and refuse him entry. We tried a few places without success, but it was getting cold, and it's no fun standing in the street, so I was just about to resign myself to an early night when I happened to remember that someone had once hinted to me that you were the man to speak to for the *really* good stuff. I made the mistake of mentioning it to Corky, who insisted we come and find you. I should never have bothered myself, since Kennington is pretty much out in the wilds, but Corky is not one to take no for an answer, so I thought I'd better tootle along with him just to make sure he didn't get into any more trouble. Anyway, we knocked on the door and couldn't get a reply, and were beginning to think we must have got the wrong place, but then we spotted your good lady wife through the window, so we knew we hadn't. She didn't reply to our knock either, so we—er—thought we'd come in anyway.'

'Through the window?' said Basil.

'The door was locked,' said Freddy, as though it were obvious. 'Still, I must say I do prefer to use the usual means of ingress and egress where possible, so if you wouldn't mind, I'd be awfully grateful if you'd open the door and let us be on our way. I have to get Corky back before his probation officer notices he's missing.'

Basil gave a humourless laugh.

'You're a one, aren't you?' he said. 'I don't know what you think you're playing at, but I don't like people breaking into my house in the middle of the night.'

'Perfectly understandable,' said Freddy. 'I beg your pardon and I promise I won't do it again.'

The apology had no effect on Basil. He levelled the gun first at Corky, then at Freddy. They both raised their hands nervously.

'I say, there's no need for that,' said Freddy, while Corky gave a bleat of agreement.

'A man's got the right to protect his own property, don't you agree?' said Basil.

'Yes, but I mean to say, there's no need to shoot us, is there? Why not simply call the police? We'll go quietly.'

'But you know about the stuff. I can't have you singing as soon as you're out of my sight.'

'Why should we do that, when we came hoping to buy some of it off you?' said Freddy.

'I don't believe you came to do anything of the sort,' said Basil. 'There are ways and means of striking a quiet deal with a fellow, and this isn't one of them. Now, if you want my guess, I should say you're both on the trail of a story, and you think you've got one in me. But I much prefer to keep my head down, so I'm afraid that's bad news for you.'

He raised the gun again.

'Stop!' said Freddy. 'You can't just shoot two people and not expect a constable to wander along with a notebook sooner or later.'

'As I said, a man has the right to protect his property,' said Basil. 'You broke in through the window, and so as far as I'm concerned, you're thieves and burglars, come to take what's mine. If I shoot you no jury will convict me—in fact, I doubt very much I'll even be charged with anything.'

'You can't be sure of that,' said Freddy.

Basil smiled briefly.

'My wife and I are well-known singers and entertainers. The public love us, and we've never had so much as a whiff of trouble before. All I have to do is turn on the charm, sing a bar or two of some of the old favourites, and I'll bet you a pound to a penny that after an hour the police will shake my hand and let me go.'

It was clear he meant every word he said. Freddy and Corky glanced at one another in fear, then back at Basil, who raised his gun.

'I'm sorry about this,' he said. 'Now—'

He got no further before there was a loud thud and a groan behind him, and he turned to see that Birdie had rolled off the sofa and was beginning to wake up. Quick as lightning, Freddy and Corky took advantage of his momentary distraction to make for the nearest exit, which happened to be the door through which Basil had arrived.

'Hi!' shouted Basil, as they slammed it behind them. There was the sound of a shot, which splintered the door and told them immediately that he had not been joking. With not a second to lose, they took the stairs two at a time and ran to the front door.

'It's locked!' said Corky.

'Quick! Upstairs!' said Freddy.

They could hear the sound of Basil cursing behind them as they turned and hared up the next flight. At the top were two doors to the left and right. In one of them—presumably Basil's bedroom—a lamp had been switched on; Freddy ran into the other, which was dark, and felt the lock for a key. There was none, and so he came out again, bumping into Corky as he did so. Basil, who was older and less fit than the other two, was halfway up the stairs. He raised the gun again. Quickly, Freddy and Corky dashed into the other bedroom and slammed the door shut. Fortunately, this one did have a key. Corky turned it and leant against the door in relief, but Freddy grabbed him by the arm and pulled him to one side—just in time, for there came the sound of another shot, and a hole appeared in the door in exactly the spot where Corky had been standing. Basil began hammering and kicking at the lock.

'Now what?' said Corky from the other side of the bed, behind which he was now crouching.

'He's going to shoot his way in any second now,' said Freddy.

He ran over to the window and threw up the sash. Below was a drop of about thirty feet into the area.

'We can't go out that way!' said Corky. 'The fall will kill us. Or we'll get impaled on the railings.'

'We'll have to go up onto the roof,' said Freddy. 'And quick. Come on!'

He was already sitting on the window-sill and preparing to climb out. Corky went pale in the face.

'What?' he said. 'Without a ladder?'

'There's a ledge here,' said Freddy. He lowered himself out. Corky came across to the window and saw that Freddy was standing precariously on a decorative moulding like a cornice just below the window, and that he was holding onto another similar one above.

'Oh, goodness,' moaned Corky.

Freddy ignored him and began to move carefully sideways. The kicking at the door became more insistent, and was followed by a loud bang. Corky gulped and shot out of the window after Freddy. Taking great care not to look down, he lowered his feet onto the narrow ledge below the window, felt for the one above it, and began to follow Freddy. Inch by inch they worked their way along the building until they reached a section which was angled into a recess. Here, some decorative brickwork on the corner gave their hands and feet easier purchase, and each paused to rest for a second before continuing. The recessed part of the building had a lower roof-line, and it was for this that Freddy was aiming. It was only a few yards away, but there was no time to lose, for just then a figure leaned out of the window through which they had just escaped, and they saw that Basil Kibble had finally got through the door and into the bedroom. He caught sight of them and gave a shout, but he did not dare shoot at them in that quiet street, for fear of attracting attention. At last Freddy reached his objective, which was another window just beneath the lower part of the roof, and stopped to wait for Corky, who was a little way behind, feeling his way along and whimpering as he went.

'Quick!' hissed Freddy. 'He'll be here in a second.'

Corky gave a moan, but went a little faster, and at last caught up. He clung to the window-frame with relief.

'Up here,' said Freddy, indicating the window. 'Climb onto the window-sill, then up onto the sash, and from there we can get onto the roof. You'd better go first.'

Corky took a deep breath and pulled himself up gingerly onto the sill, then reached up and grasped the cornicing that ran around the edge of the roof parapet. The window-frame splintered slightly when he stood on it, but a few seconds later he was over and safe. Not a minute too soon, for just then a light went on in the room beyond the window. Freddy started and nearly lost his footing, but quickly regained his balance and made a grab for the parapet. Through the glass he could see Basil, not eight inches away, struggling with the catch. Freddy climbed up after Corky, just as the window opened and a hand reached out. It grabbed at his ankle, but he kicked out and shook it off, and with one last enormous heave was on the roof. The two of them collapsed, panting.

'What do we do now?' said Corky. 'Wait for a passing dirigible?'

Freddy looked about him. They were sitting in the lead gutter between two pitched roofs. Over the parapet in front of them was the way they had just come. He stood up and followed the gutter to the back of the house. It ended in a drain-pipe, which fell vertically for about twenty feet, then bent to avoid an outhouse and continued to the ground.

'We can't go down there,' said Corky next to him. 'We'll end up in their back garden and be back where we started.'

'Then we shall just have to try next door,' said Freddy, indicating the roof to his left.

'Must we?'

'Do you have a better idea?'

Corky sighed, and followed Freddy across the roof to the next gutter. The moon had risen, and they could see out across the rooftops of London, but there was no time to stop and admire the view. Freddy was already peering down into the yard of the house at the end of the terrace, and testing the drain-pipe.

'I think we might do it,' he said. 'You go first.'

'But you'll fall on me,' said Corky.

'Don't be an ass. All right, then, go second if you like.'

'No!' said Corky, and hastened forward. 'If I fall, you'll tell them to write me a decent obituary, won't you?' he said, as he lowered himself carefully over the edge.

'No, I shall tell them to be sure and say what a plague upon mankind you were.'

'You wouldn't!'

'You'll never know, so if I were you I should hold on good and tight,' said Freddy.

Corky grumbled and let himself down. Fearful that the pipe might come away from the wall if they both climbed down it at once, Freddy waited until Corky had arrived safely on the roof of the out-house before starting. At last they were both safely on the ground, and to their joy found that the door in the garden wall, which they had tried before from the street side, was only bolted. Within seconds they were free, and hurrying towards Waterloo in search of a taxi.

'Well, that was a splendid little adventure,' said Corky, who had quite recovered his spirits. 'It ought to make a big splash in tomorrow's evening edition.'

'Yes,' said Freddy. 'I suppose the Kibbles will make a bolt for it now. Or do you think they might try and brazen it out? After all, we did break in, and that won't look good in the eyes of the police.'

'They can try all they want, but we've got the stuff,' said Corky smugly. He patted his pocket. 'The evidence is here, and they can't deny it now.'

'We'd better take it to the police,' said Freddy. 'Where's the nearest station?'

'Ah, yes,' said Corky. 'That's another thing.'

He stopped and looked around him in exaggerated fashion, then tapped his nose and drew Freddy into a doorway.

'What do you say to it, then?' he said. He brought the parcel of cocaine out of his pocket and weighed it in his hand. 'I should say there was a good half a pound here. An ounce for you and an ounce for me, and the police can have the rest.'

'What are you talking about?' said Freddy.

'They'll never know. Consider it a bonus payment for the overtime we've done this evening.'

Freddy eyed him in astonishment.

'Are you suggesting we *steal* this cocaine?' he said. 'You? Corky Beckwith? The scourge of every drug fiend from Isleworth to Ilford? The crusader for morality who has vowed to eradicate the epidemic of dope that is destroying our nation's youth?'

'Oh, pish,' said Corky. 'One has to maintain appearances for the sake of the paper, but what a man does in private is his own business.'

He peered into the packet, took a large pinch and snuffed it delicately, then gave a sigh of satisfaction.

'I should say this was the good stuff, all right,' he said.

'You rotten hypocrite!' said Freddy, outraged. 'After all the things you've written, and all those people you've hounded.'

'Never mind them—they deserved it. Look, do take a bit. You've done some rather good work this evening, and there'll be plenty left over for our story.'

'But I don't want any.'

Corky leered.

'Don't try and pretend to be holier than thou, Freddy. I can see right through you. I know you're craving the dope—you as good as told me so today.'

'No I didn't. When did I say that?'

'Why, this morning, when you told me of this friend of yours down in the country. Naturally, I saw through your ruse immediately. You were talking about yourself, of course.'

'No I wasn't!' exclaimed Freddy.

'Oh, come, now. How green do you suppose I am? It was perfectly obvious whom you meant. Now, it's clear you don't trust me not to tell, but I should have thought that this evening's little adventure would have convinced you that I'm a man of my word. You can't say I didn't produce the goods, can you? I've done you a favour and handed you a story that ought to put you in old Bickerstaffe's good books for weeks. Don't worry—I shan't insist you squeal on all your little pals who spend their weekends face-down in the white powder with you, but if I were you I'd keep my share of this haul to myself. After all, you deserve it.'

'Look here,' said Freddy, who was becoming impatient. 'You'd better forget all this nonsense. I don't want any of it, and I'm not letting you keep it either, since it seems you can't be trusted with it. I'll take it to the police. Give it to me.'

'Certainly not,' said Corky. 'Fair's fair.'

'But it's evidence,' said Freddy.

He made as if to take the package from Corky.

'Hi!' said Corky indignantly, and held it out of his reach. There followed an unseemly tussle.

'Oh, *there*, then,' said Corky petulantly at last. He stood back, and Freddy was left holding the packet. 'I suppose you're going to go to the police now.'

'Well, better I than you, fathead,' said Freddy. 'At least I haven't just taken a faceful of the stuff, and can tell them what happened in a calm and rational manner.'

'A calm and rational manner, eh? We'll see about that,' said Corky.

Before Freddy could say a word, he stepped forward, grabbed Freddy by the hair with one hand and plunged his other into the packet, then rubbed a fistful of cocaine viciously into Freddy's face and up his nose. Freddy gave a strangled bellow and wrenched himself free.

'Why, you—you—' he spluttered, wiping at his face.

'Let's see what the police say when you turn up giggling like an escaped lunatic, with half the dope in your hands and the other half all over your clothes,' said Corky spitefully. 'I'm sure they'll be *delighted* to listen to your story.'

Freddy directed a number of unrepeatable words at him, but Corky merely gave a supercilious smile and looked at his watch.

'It's not quite four,' he said. 'Shall we say ten o'clock at the Yard? That ought to give you time to sleep it off. Mind, don't be late!'

And with that he made his escape. Freddy brushed himself down as best he could, fuming, and wondered what to do next. He still had the packet, and briefly considered going to the police anyway, but swiftly abandoned the idea, for he suspected he should only babble. He felt extremely wide awake, but it was too late to go out, since everything would be closed now—and in any case, he was filthy after his climb over the rooftops—so he went home, where he was suddenly assailed by an overwhelming urge to write a novel based upon his experiences of that evening. It was somehow vitally important that he put his ideas down now, before he forget them, and so he fetched out his typewriter and dashed off five chapters at great speed in two hours, before collapsing on the sofa and falling asleep just as dawn was breaking.

Chapter Eighteen

'BASIL AND BIRDIE, eh?' said Sergeant Bird. 'Who'd have thought it? Any sign of them yet?'

'Not a one,' said Inspector Entwistle. 'They've skipped it, all right. We'll watch the ports, but I doubt they've got that far, if she really is in the condition these two chaps described.'

'Sounds like she needs a hospital more than anything else,' observed Bird.

'That's an idea. I wonder—have them make inquiries in private nursing-homes hereabouts. He might have parked her in one of them before he made a run for it.'

'Good at dressing up, too, these actors,' said Bird. 'I shouldn't wonder if he'd gone in disguise.'

'Well, that will make our job all the harder,' said the inspector. He frowned. 'What about these reporters? I don't know that I believe their story.'

'It's a strange one,' said Bird. 'Running around over the rooftops at night with bags of dope. Sounds like high jinks to me.'

'I had half a mind to arrest them both on a charge of disorderly behaviour,' said Entwistle.

'But they did bring us the stuff,' said Bird reasonably.

'They did, but why did they take so long about it? If you ask me, they had a go at it themselves first, to look at the state of them when they came in.'

'What about this second packet of coke? The one Pilkington-Soames said had been planted on a friend of his at the Maypole during a fight. He wouldn't name the friend, but he seemed to think that it must have been Kibble who did the planting.'

'It makes sense, I suppose,' said the inspector grudgingly. 'If the police arrived and started arresting people he wouldn't want to be caught with it on him. And the two lots are of the same quality, according to the lab chaps.'

'Did Dacres get her supply from Kibble, then, d'you think?'

'I imagine so,' said Entwistle. 'Although hers was of much lower quality.'

'Different batches, presumably,' said Bird.

Entwistle pursed his lips.

'There's something fishy going on with those two reporters, I'm sure of it. I don't believe for a moment that they got in through an open window.'

'Well, they're hardly likely to admit it if they did break in,' said Bird. 'Still, we have had trouble with Beckwith before. He's known in the force as a bit of a pest, and some of the stories he writes are just this side of libellous. Pilkington-Soames we know from the Maltravers case, of course.'

'Yes,' said Entwistle. 'And that was never cleared up to our satisfaction either.'

'He did help to catch the killer, in a manner of speaking,' said the sergeant.

'I suppose so. At any rate, whether this Kennington story is true or not, the Kibbles have certainly disappeared, and there are signs that shots were fired in the house, so I should like very much to speak to them—if we can ever find them.'

'It's a pity, really,' said Bird ruminatively. 'They were a funny couple. But it just goes to show you can't trust anyone these days.'

'It changes things somewhat in the Dacres case, too,' said the inspector. 'The Kibbles are suspects now, thanks to this drugs angle. If they were supplying her with cocaine, and she threatened to expose them, then who's to say they didn't decide to take matters into their own hands and silence her once and for all?'

'Do you think that's what happened, sir?' said Bird.

'Well, we know Dacres was the sort to throw her weight around a bit and make enemies. What if the Kibbles had crossed her in some way? She wasn't the type to stand for it without retaliating—or, at least, threatening to retaliate.'

'Do we know whether either of them had the opportunity that evening?' said Bird.

Entwistle referred to his notes.

'Difficult to tell,' he said. 'We know they were at the piano most of the evening, but they stopped for a rest when Miss Dacres made her grand announcement. Birdie was seen talking to Sir Aldridge Featherstone for a good while after that, but we don't know where Basil went. We do know they were both back at the piano by about ten past eleven.'

'But we still don't know at exactly what time Dorothy Dacres died,' said Bird.

'No, and that's what makes it so difficult—we don't know what led up to her death. If it was done on the spur of the moment after a row, then the murderer would have been missing for several minutes. But if the whole thing was planned in advance, it would have taken a matter of seconds to sneak up on her and tip her over the edge.'

'True. We still don't know whether it was premeditated or not, assuming it *was* murder.'

'I think we must assume it was,' said Entwistle. 'There are too many people with motives running around, and there's too little reason for it to have been an accident or suicide.'

'Proving it will be nigh on impossible, though, unless we can find a witness or get a confession.'

'Yes,' said Entwistle thoughtfully.

'Supposing it wasn't Basil Kibble,' said Bird. 'Who did it? Robert Kenrick?'

'Perhaps. He certainly had the opportunity, and the motive, too.'

'You don't seem convinced, sir,' said the sergeant.

'I'm not,' said the inspector. 'He doesn't strike me as the type. He's very much an innocent abroad, don't you think?'

'True. But even the most honest man might do something desperate if driven to it. And he seemed very cut up when he thought he was going to lose his girl because of Dacres.'

'Well, looking at it logically he's the most likely, since he was on the terrace before eleven and disappeared entirely after that, so I won't strike him off the list just yet, but it will take a lot more to convince me,' said Entwistle. 'Now, Cora Drucker. She didn't have much opportunity to do it, since everyone agrees she was wandering around in the living-room, asking people whether they'd seen Kenrick. Incidentally, do we know what she wanted to speak to him about?'

'I don't think she mentioned it, sir,' said Bird.

'Hmm. Perhaps we'd better ask her. Now, what motive? Jealousy?'

'Possible. She was an actress once, but gave it up when her sister started taking up all the limelight.'

'Thwarted ambition,' said Entwistle. 'That might be reason enough to commit murder, but since it doesn't seem as though she had the opportunity, we'll leave her aside for the moment. Now, Eugene Penk. He and Kenneth Neale give each other an alibi, at least for the first part of the half-hour period, while Sarah Rowland is his alibi for the rest of the time, since she's quite certain he didn't come in from the smaller terrace until the news got out about the incident.'

'What was his motive?'

'Any or none. We know he and Dacres were married but separated, but since he claims they'd agreed to divorce, I don't see the sense in his throwing her off the balcony purely to get rid of a wife he no longer wanted. These Americans divorce each other at the drop of a hat, as far as I understand it, so murder would be completely unnecessary.'

'Might there have been another reason for it? On the business side, I mean. He didn't sound any too keen to have her in his picture, although he had to make the best of it.'

'Yes, it looks as though he's saddled himself with the worst sort of business partner—one who has all the money but none of the knowledge, and thinks he ought to have a say in how the business is run despite having no idea of what he's doing.'

'I gather Sir Aldridge Featherstone is putting some money into the company now,' said Bird.

'True, but Dorothy Dacres was still a thorn in Penk's side for this particular picture. Her being given the part offended a lot of people, which would have made things difficult for him. Several people seemed to think she was completely wrong for the rôle and would spoil the film—and it was very important that this picture succeed, after his previous ones flopped. That sounds like enough of a motive to me. But he doesn't appear to have had the opportunity, so we shall have to leave him for now.'

'Kenneth Neale, then?' suggested Bird. 'Penk had persuaded him into directing the film on the understanding that Augusta Laing would play the part of Helen Harper, and he was furious when he found out that he'd been tricked.'

'Yes, but as you pointed out before, he'd be far more likely to have chucked Penk off a balcony rather than Dorothy Dacres. I mean to say, I can't find any evidence that he had a particular grudge against Dorothy herself.'

'I hear she was rude to his daughter,' said the sergeant.

'That's not reason enough to kill someone, surely?'

'You'd be surprised,' said Bird. 'People can be funny about their little darlings.'

'In that case, doesn't Mrs. Neale have a motive too?'

'She was with Ada all evening,' said Bird. 'And I doubt very much whether a seven-year-old would keep quiet if she saw her mother throw another woman off a terrace.'

'Probably not,' agreed the inspector. 'Now, Seymour Cosgrove. Arrested the other night at the Maypole for being drunk and attacking Pilkington-Soames.'

'He seems to attract a lot of that sort of thing, Mr. Pilkington-Soames does,' observed the sergeant.

'He's a trouble-maker if ever I saw one,' said Entwistle. 'It's just lucky for him he doesn't have any motive that I can see for killing Dacres, or I'd have something to say to him. But it appears that in this case he was the innocent party—or, shall we say, he didn't start the fight. Presumably he must have done something to offend, though, if Cosgrove felt obliged to swing at him.'

'What does Cosgrove say about the night at the Abingdon?'

The inspector grunted.

'I didn't make much progress there,' he said. 'He still claims he can't remember exactly where he was during the half-hour in question, but was wandering around the living-room talking to people. Mrs. Neale remembers speaking to him at about eleven, but that was only for a few minutes. There's a good quarter of an hour before that unaccounted for, and another quarter of an hour afterwards.'

'He's the one who lost his job, isn't he?'

'Yes. And we have a number of witnesses to say he didn't take it at all well. Whether he took it badly enough to kill is another matter, though.'

'Good photographer, is he, this chap?'

'Supposedly. He does all the artistic stuff—you know, pictures of society women wrapped in cellophane with cats on their head, that sort of thing. Not my idea of art, but he seems to be well thought of.'

'Ah, these artistic types,' said Bird, understanding. 'They can be a bit temperamental.'

'And this one doesn't have an alibi,' said Entwistle. 'But again, the proof's the thing. Now, Augusta Laing. She's our last, and I can't find out what she was doing either. She went missing shortly after the announcement, and turned up again just before eleven, when she went out onto the balcony with Pilkington-Soames. They stayed outside for a few minutes with Miss Drucker, then they all went in together and Miss Laing was in view from then until Dacres was found.'

'Dorothy Dacres didn't vanish until after ten to eleven, so that doesn't give her long to do the deed,' said the sergeant. 'Less then ten minutes, in fact.'

'True, but if she was already waiting on the terrace when Dacres came out, it would have been easy enough. Still, I don't really think she did it. This doesn't seem like a woman's crime to me—far too violent.'

'Yes,' said Bird. 'Anyone else? What about Sir Aldridge Featherstone?'

'He's an outsider, but I suppose we oughtn't to discount him. I can't see what his motive would have been, unless it was similar to that of Penk's, and he was worried about the effect Dacres would have on the film. But I understand the definitive agreement for him to take shares in Aston-Penk wasn't signed until after Dacres' death. It seems a little far-fetched to me to think that a respectable business-man like Sir Aldridge Featherstone should operate in that way. I mean to say, surely if he didn't like the presence of Dorothy Dacres in the film, he would simply refuse his backing rather than chuck her off a roof?'

'It would be a queer way of going about things,' agreed the sergeant. A thought struck him. 'Look here,' he said. 'Don't you think we've missed someone out? What about Miss Rowland? Might she have had the opportunity? She certainly disliked Dacres enough.'

'Yes, I had thought of her already,' said Entwistle, nodding, 'but I think we can safely eliminate her. She was seen by many people that evening—but even if that weren't the case, she's given us such specific and detailed information about everybody's movements from moment to moment that I can't imagine she'd have had the time to nip out and kill Dacres, since she was much too busy watching everyone else.'

'True,' said Bird, slightly crestfallen.

'No,' said Entwistle, 'I think we have to admit that Basil Kibble is by far our most likely suspect at the moment. I only hope the chaps catch him quickly.'

'I'm sure they'll find him sooner or later,' said Bird. 'These actors don't like staying out of the spotlight for long. He'll turn up again, you mark my words.'

CHAPTER NINETEEN

FOR THE NEXT few days, Freddy basked in his triumph at the part he had played in exposing Basil and Birdie's illegal activities. The Kibbles' disappearance had allowed him to stretch the story out over several days, and there was much speculation among the public as to where they might have gone. Reports came in of possible sightings from all over the country, and Freddy heard that the indefatigable Corky Beckwith had been haring about from Cornwall to Yorkshire, following up all of them, in his determination to be the one to catch the fugitives. Freddy was wanted on another story, and so could not join in the chase—much to his annoyance, for he knew Corky would not hesitate to crow when they next met. The *Herald* had dedicated a great deal of space to the 'high society drug scandal,' as it called it, and Freddy, to his great indignation, had read several stories in which Corky claimed all the credit for the discovery for himself, and hinted strongly that a rival reporter had nearly ruined everything through his own incompetence. By Wednesday, however, the clamour had started to die down, although the Kibbles still had not been found. Freddy wondered whether Basil would be arrested for the murder of Dorothy Dacres when he was eventually caught, for it seemed that here was a possible motive for her death— and Basil had certainly showed that he was prepared to use violence in order to avoid discovery. But since he and his wife had vanished without trace, no further progress could made on the case at present.

On Wednesday afternoon Gussie called.

'Are you busy?' she said. 'If not, come and take me out to tea.'

She was looking very chic in a smart hat and coat, and greeted Freddy as cheerfully as ever when they met.

'How's your jaw?' she said, as they sat down at their table. 'Better, I hope.'

'Yes, thanks,' said Freddy. 'Luckily it wasn't broken.'

'Look here, I'm sorry about that night at the Maypole,' she said. 'I was awfully squiffy, I'm afraid, and I wanted to annoy Seymour, but I never dreamed he'd land you one. Please say you forgive me.'

She gazed at him appealingly, eyes wide.

'Of course I forgive you,' said Freddy. 'You weren't the one who thumped me, were you?'

'No, but it was my fault he did. Poor Seymour—it's so terribly easy to work him up.'

'He's not still in gaol, is he?'

'No. I sent Ken to pay the fine, as Seymour hasn't a bean, and most likely couldn't have paid it himself. That's why he was so angry at what Dorothy did, you see. He's terribly well respected in Britain, and works so very hard, but he's useless at asking for money, and so people rather take advantage. This job with the magazine was a tremendous opportunity, and they were simply throwing dollars at him, so he'd never have had to ask for it or send a bill. Now he's back where he started.'

'Is there no chance of his getting the job now?'

'I don't think so, because they've offered it to someone else instead. And what makes it worse is that it's Dickie Sanders. The two of them fell out a few years ago, and it sticks in Seymour's throat to lose a job to him.'

'You're very fond of him, aren't you?' said Freddy.

'Oh, I'm quite desperately in love with him,' said Gussie. 'But he infuriates me so with his high-handedness that I had to give him the chuck before I laid into him with a half-brick.'

'Gussie,' said Freddy suddenly. 'Where were you on the night Dorothy died? I mean, where did you go after she made her announcement?'

She looked down, then back up quickly.

'Where do you think I was, you idiot?' she said at last. 'I was out on the landing in a flood of tears, of course. But I should have died rather than let anyone see me at it, so I stayed there until I'd got hold of myself. Seymour came out and found me, as a matter of fact, and we had another row.'

'What about?'

'I *think* he was trying to comfort me, but he went about it completely the wrong way. Then he stormed off, and—and—'

'And what?'

'That's just it,' she whispered. 'I don't know. I don't know where he went after he left me. And I've been so terribly afraid ever since that he might have done something stupid.'

Freddy remembered Seymour's words on the night of the party. 'Someone's going to murder that woman one day,' he had said. Had he taken matters into his own hands in order to make his prediction come true?

'At what time did he leave you?' he said.

'Why, I don't know. When did I come back in and talk to you?'

'Just before eleven, I think.'

'Then it must have been a minute or so before that,' she said. 'The silly ass did me one favour at least—he exasperated me so much that I couldn't think about crying any more, and so I went back into the party almost as soon as he'd gone.'

'I saw him talking to Penk just as the hotel manager arrived, after everybody had rushed onto the terrace, thinking there'd been a motor accident out in the street,' said Freddy. 'He didn't want to look—said it was ghoulish.'

'Then that's twenty minutes or more unaccounted for,' said Gussie. 'I wish I knew where he'd gone.'

'Have you asked him?'

'No,' she said. 'We're not strictly on speaking terms, so I couldn't.'

'Perhaps it doesn't matter where he was,' said Freddy. 'I mean, now that this new information about the Kibbles has come to light. It looks as though Dorothy's cocaine came from Basil, and once the police find him I expect they'll arrest him for murder too.'

'Do you really think so?' said Gussie. 'Was it Basil who killed her, then?'

'I couldn't say, but his behaviour has certainly been suspicious enough. I'm fairly sure it was he who planted the cocaine on you at the Maypole, at any rate. When the police arrived he was frightened they'd start searching everybody, so he put the dope in the first place he could think of.'

'Oh, goodness!' exclaimed Gussie. 'I believe you're right. I remember now—my bag was on the chair next to him. It would have been as easy as anything for him to have shoved it in there on the spur of the moment.' Her face fell. 'But that doesn't necessarily mean he killed Dorothy, does it?'

'No,' said Freddy.

She toyed forlornly with a spoon.

'I do wish Seymour and I hadn't rowed that night,' she said in a small voice. 'I should so like to know where he was for that half an hour. I dare say I'll never find out now. Perhaps I'll never even see him again.'

'I'm not so sure about that,' said Freddy with a start, for he had just seen Seymour Cosgrove himself come in through the door of the café. He moved his chair back and glanced about hurriedly, looking for an easy means of escape, but there was none. Seymour made a bee-line for their table and stood before them.

'Hallo,' he said.

Freddy was relieved to see he was looking much less hostile than he had on the night at the Maypole.

'Seymour! What are you doing here? Did you follow me?' exclaimed Gussie indignantly. 'How dare you?'

'I couldn't help it. I was outside your house, making up my mind to knock, when I saw—' he indicated Freddy. 'Too late again, I suppose. I know I oughtn't to have followed, but I'd made up my mind to talk to you and I won't funk it, although I should far rather have done it in private.'

'Talk to me about what?'

'I don't—' he paused uncomfortably. 'If you must know, I wanted to apologize to you.'

'You did, did you?' said Gussie. 'What did you want to apologize for?'

'For being a fool. I don't know what got into me. I'm sorry, Gussie.'

'Oh,' she said, a little mollified. 'Well, then. But I think you ought to apologize to Freddy first.'

'What?'

She stared at him imperiously down her nose. He stuck his chin out.

'All right, then,' he said grudgingly at last to Freddy. 'I'm sorry I punched you. But you were kissing my girl.'

'Only because I asked him to,' said Gussie.

'Yes, well I could hardly punch you, could I?' said Seymour.

'I should think not! Very well, if you promise you'll behave you may sit down.'

Seymour took a seat gingerly. Freddy turned his chair a little more, so as to allow for a quick escape should it prove necessary, but Seymour did not seem inclined to continue the fight. The three of them sat in an uncomfortable silence for several seconds, then Freddy said with some trepidation:

'Aren't you going to ask him?'

'You ask him,' said Gussie.

'What, and get another biff on the chin for my pains? No thanks.'

'Ask me what?' said Seymour in surprise, looking from one to the other of them.

Gussie hesitated, but there was no going back now.

'Seymour,' she said, twisting her hands together. 'Do you remember the night Dorothy died?'

'Of course I do,' he replied.

'And you found me on the landing and we had a row.'

'Look, I'm sorry about that,' he said quickly. 'I didn't mean to upset you.'

'Yes, yes, never mind that,' she said. She hesitated, then said all in a rush, 'Where did you go after you left me?' He stared, and she went on hurriedly, 'It's just that nobody seems to have seen you after that, and I—I've been awfully afraid that you— that you might have—'

'Might have what?' he said. Then he seemed to realize what she meant, and his eyes widened. 'You don't mean to say you think I went off and chucked Dorothy over the edge, do you?'

'I don't know,' she whispered. 'You were so very angry with her, and then Ada said she'd overheard you threatening to kill her. I was *almost* sure you hadn't meant it, but I thought—I thought—'

'Well, you can stop thinking about it,' he said firmly. 'I was furious with Dorothy that night because she started laughing at me again about the magazine. She still hadn't understood what she'd done, and thought I ought to laugh about it too. Well, I didn't. I told her exactly what I thought of her. I dare say I might even have threatened to kill her, but it's one thing to say something like that in the heat of anger and quite another to do it—and I assure you I didn't. If you want to know where I was after I left you, I went into the maid's room with Bob Kenrick. He'd had a row with his girl too, and we both needed bucking up, so I nabbed a bottle of whisky off the table at the side of the room, and we went and sat down for a drink and a smoke and some peace and quiet—although we weren't there long because then all the commotion started. I didn't say anything because he didn't mention it, and I thought perhaps he didn't want it getting around that he'd been upset. I'd have spoken up if necessary, of course, but the police didn't press the matter so I kept quiet. You didn't really think I killed Dorothy, did you?'

'Not really,' said Gussie. 'I mean, I hoped so very much you hadn't, but I couldn't help thinking that perhaps you'd seen I was upset after losing the part, and that you'd gone and done something rash.'

'Oh, Gussie, how could you?' said Seymour. He reached out and clasped her hand. 'I promise you I didn't do it. Please tell me you believe me. It would kill me if I thought you didn't.'

'Yes, yes, of course I believe you!' said Gussie eagerly. 'How could I have doubted you? Oh, Seymour, I'm sorry I was angry with you.'

'You had every right to be. I know I've been an ass, but it's only because I adore you so.'

They seemed to have completely forgotten Freddy's existence. Freddy blew out his cheeks and stared hard at the wall as they leaned towards one another, gazing deeply into each other's eyes.

'Promise me you don't doubt me,' said Seymour. 'Tell me again you know I didn't kill Dorothy.'

'Of course I know it, and I was a fool to have thought it even for a second,' said Gussie. There was a pause, then she lowered her voice and whispered, 'But *would* you have done it if I'd asked you to? Would you have done it for me?'

He fixed her with a look of great intensity.

'You know I'd do anything for you, my darling,' he said.

'Oh, Seymour,' she breathed.

Then suddenly there was a crash of crockery and teaspoons as they lunged at one another and started kissing madly across the table. Freddy counted slowly to twenty, but they did not appear inclined to stop, and so in the end he stood up and left quietly, consoling himself that at least one of his questions had been answered. Not that they seemed to care, but it now looked as though neither Gussie nor Seymour could have killed Dorothy Dacres.

CHAPTER TWENTY

ALTHOUGH THINGS WERE quiet for the next day or so, Freddy still could not get the Dorothy Dacres case out of his mind. He was relieved that Gussie had not done it—a possibility which had been worrying him for some time—while Seymour Cosgrove also appeared to have an alibi of sorts, if he really had been in the maid's room with Robert Kenrick after eleven o'clock, since there was no way of getting onto the terrace from there. In that case, assuming Basil had not done it—and Freddy was by no means convinced he had—now that Gussie and Seymour seemed to have been exonerated, it looked rather as though the only person who had been in the right place at the right time was Robert Kenrick himself, for he had been out on the terrace for a good twenty minutes at around the same time that Dorothy had gone missing. Until they knew when Dorothy had died, they would not know exactly when an alibi was needed for, but it could not be denied that Kenrick's presence on the terrace at the right time looked very suspicious. Freddy could not help remembering the conversation he had overheard between Dorothy and Kenrick, in which it sounded very much as though she were threatening him, and realized he had never yet mentioned it to the police. He supposed he ought to do so, although the idea made him uncomfortable, since he knew Kenrick must already be under suspicion given his lack of an alibi. Somehow he could not see Robert Kenrick as a murderer, for he lacked the ruthlessness that seemed to lie behind Dorothy's death. That would not prevent the police from arresting him, however, if they found any other evidence to support the theory—always assuming there were any such evidence to be found, for whoever the killer was, he had hidden his tracks well, and had left no trace of his crime.

There was nothing to be done at present, but Freddy was restless, and had a nagging feeling that the answer to the mystery lay at the Abingdon. He was almost certain he had overlooked an obvious clue, and so he left his desk and went to Mayfair, with no particular purpose in mind but to stand and stare at the hotel in case some idea should strike him. There was a bustle of people coming and going when he arrived, and it occurred to him that the recent dramatic events here must have been good for business. A number of people had bene-fited from the death of Dorothy Dacres. Surely it could not have been an accident, since her demise appeared to have helped so many? It seemed far too much of a coincidence to be possible.

He was still gazing at the hotel entrance when a taxi drew up outside the door, and out of it stepped the Neales, with their daughter Adorable Ada. The little girl waved when she saw him.

'Hallo,' she said, as he crossed the street to join them. 'We're going in to tea. Mummy, look, it's that man. The one with the funny face.'

'Don't be rude, darling,' said Mrs. Neale. 'People can't help the way they look. Hallo, you're Augusta's friend Freddy, aren't you?'

Freddy acknowledged that he was.

'I was supposed to be meeting someone here,' he said on the spur of the moment, 'but she hasn't turned up.'

'Oh, what a pity,' said Patience. 'Perhaps you'd like to join us instead. My husband has come to see Mr. Penk, and we tagged along as we had nothing else to do, but the men will be talking about all sorts of dull stuff that we don't care about, so you're welcome to come and sit with us if you like.'

'Oh, yes, yes,' agreed Kenneth Neale, on a nudge from his wife.

Freddy indicated that he should like nothing better, and they went in. Once in the opulent hotel lounge, they sat in deep-cushioned chairs and listened to a string quartet, while Ada gazed about her with distant interest. Kenneth Neale, who, in his slightly shabby suit, looked out of place against the tasteful surroundings, was just glancing at his watch and beginning to remark on the time-keeping of Hollywood folk, when Eugene Penk strode in, accompanied by Cora Drucker. As always, Penk looked unmistakably American in his air and his dress, while his stocky build and fighter's stance spoke clearly of a man who meant business. His eyebrows were drawn together in an expression of great purpose, until he caught sight of Neale and his expression relaxed. He came over, grasped the director in a firm handshake, and immediately began talking of money, then the two men wandered off to sit at another table, leaving Cora Drucker to sit down with the remaining group. Freddy was surprised at the change in her since he had last seen her. He had noted her as a pretty girl but not much more, for her beauty had been eclipsed by that of her sister, of whom she had seemed but a pale imitation. Now, however, with Dorothy's death, it looked as though she had emerged to shine in her own right. She was dressed in an emerald green afternoon dress which was cut to a nicety and flattered both her complexion and her figure. Her hair was smooth and glossy, and her skin without flaw, and she almost glowed. What a change! Was Cora another person who had seen Dorothy Dacres' death as an opportunity rather than a tragedy? It certainly seemed so, for although she spoke with apparent sincerity of the trials of the past week or two, there was no denying that she had blossomed in quite spectacular fashion.

They talked of this and that, and at length Penk and Neale returned to rejoin the party. Freddy immediately noticed that Penk and Cora appeared to be on very friendly terms, for he sat next to her and every so often they exchanged glances of confidence. It soon emerged that Cora Drucker had made up her mind to return to acting, and that Eugene Penk fully supported her decision—indeed, had begun to look for parts for her.

'I've never done a talkie,' she said to Freddy, 'but I started out in the theatre, so I guess nobody will complain about my voice.'

Freddy made a suitable reply, then said:

'This is a sudden decision, isn't it? I mean to say, I understood you'd retired from acting.'

'I had,' she replied. 'Or at least, I thought I had. But now—well, there's no use in pretending—I won't have to suffer all those comparisons to Dorothy that I used to get. Everyone admired her so much, and I couldn't help feeling that they looked at her and then at me, and found me wanting. It hurt my confidence, and it must have shown, because I stopped getting parts. That just made me feel worse, and so in the end I had to stop. But Eugene is very kind, and says I never ought to have given up in the first place, and he's convinced me to try again.'

Freddy noticed she kept touching Penk's arm affectionately as she spoke, and did his best not to raise his eyebrows. He knew, of course, that Eugene Penk and Dorothy Dacres had been secretly married, but now that Penk was a free man, had he and Cora taken the opportunity to strike up a closer friendship?

Penk now leaned across.

'So you're the man who found out who killed Dorothy,' he said without preamble.

'Well, that's not quite certain yet,' replied Freddy. 'I don't think there's any solid evidence to connect Basil to her death.'

'Evidence or not, it's pretty clear he did it,' said Penk. 'I hear you had a narrow escape across the rooftops.'

'We did,' said Freddy. 'Not the easiest way to get from the front of a building to the back, but when one's being chased by a man with a gun one doesn't have much choice.'

Here he was called upon to tell the story of his adventures, which he did with only a small amount of exaggeration.

'Do you think they'll catch them?' said Patience Neale.

'I expect they will, my dear,' said her husband. 'They're too well known to hide for long. Someone is bound to recognize them.'

'Poor Birdie,' she said. 'And she was so looking forward to filming her part in *For Every Yesterday*. I suppose that's all off now.'

'Is the film still going ahead?' said Freddy.

'It sure is,' said Penk cheerfully. 'I'd rather it remained confidential for the moment—you know, so soon after what happened—but we expect to begin production in January, with Augusta Laing playing the part of Helen Harper.'

Freddy glanced at Kenneth Neale, who said humorously:

'You'd better offer her the part first.'

Penk waved a hand.

'She won't say no. And if she does, we can find somebody else.'

'I'll see to it she doesn't say no,' said Neale. 'In fact, I'll telephone her as soon as we get home.'

He looked very pleased with himself—and no wonder, thought Freddy, for now he had the actress he had always wanted for the part.

'I'm going to America,' said Adorable Ada to Freddy. She was sitting next to him and had been staring at him fixedly for several minutes.

'Are you, indeed?' he said. 'Shall you make films there?'

'I think so,' she replied. 'Daddy has been talking to Mr. Penk about it. They say I shall be a star. I hope I shall like America.

Everyone there is very rich and beautiful. I hope I'm good enough.'

There was just a touch of anxiety in her tone. It was the first time Freddy had ever seen her demonstrate the slightest self-doubt. Perhaps she was human after all.

'I'm sure you will be,' he said. 'But you can always stop acting if you're not having fun. I dare say there will be lots of children for you to play with in America.'

'I don't know any children,' she said thoughtfully. 'I wonder what they're like.'

Freddy wanted to say, 'Much like you, I expect,' but that was so patently unlikely that he held his tongue.

'It's a pity I don't have any brothers or sisters,' went on Ada. 'Then I should have someone to play with. I should like a sister, I think.'

'Should you?'

'Yes. Then I should know there was at least *one* person who liked me. Cora was Dorothy's sister, you know, and I think she must have liked her, even if no-one else did.'

She looked a little wistful, and Freddy almost felt sorry for her, since she evidently had no friends her own age.

'If I had a sister, then she could arrange surprises for me, like Cora did for Dorothy,' she went on. 'I like surprises. Cakes and dolls, and other things. Do you like surprises?'

'As long as they're nice ones,' said Freddy. He was slightly distracted, for he had just had an idea and was trying to remember what it was, and he was also trying to hear something Eugene Penk was saying about his business partner, Henry Aston, who had apparently been inconsolable at Dorothy's death, since he had been very fond of her personally.

'Henry's a swell guy,' said Penk, 'but he gets carried away by his enthusiasms. I guess he's so rich he can afford to do it, but I told him that's no way to run a business. Why, if I'd let him, he'd have given Dorothy the lead part in every one of our pictures, and then wondered why they all failed. He's as shrewd a man as you could ever hope to meet when it comes to factories and railroads, but he's new to the movie business and a little confused by it. He thinks making a picture is as simple a matter as laying a length of track here or making so many farm machines per week there. He doesn't understand yet that movie stars aren't made of springs and metal, and that you can't make them do what you want just by snapping your fingers.'

He then held forth about Sir Aldridge, and the opportunities to be had from a closer partnership between British and American film companies, and was most complimentary about the talent of British directors and actors. He seemed to be making every effort to win back the little ground he had lost with Kenneth Neale—and it looked as though it were working, since the Neales were now apparently planning to go to Hollywood to try their luck there, with the support of Penk.

Shortly after that, the little party broke up, and Freddy headed back to Fleet Street. He had hoped to find out something useful that afternoon, but he had learned nothing, except that everybody was happier since Dorothy's death—of which he had already been well aware. He frowned, for he was still convinced that the answer to the mystery lay at the hotel; moreover, he was irked, because he was almost sure he had said something very clever not half an hour ago, but he could not for the life of him remember what it was. He shook his head in frustration, then made up his mind to stop thinking about it. Perhaps it would come back to him sooner or later—he certainly hoped so, for the trail was going cold, and without new evidence it was starting to look as though the mystery would never be solved.

Chapter Twenty-One

NEWS CAME THE next day that Basil and Birdie Kibble had been caught in an attempt to flee to France. As suspected, they had been in disguise, travelling as an elderly couple, and had made a concerted effort to resist arrest. In the end they had been subdued, however, and brought back to London, where they were currently being questioned. When Freddy heard this, he went along to Scotland Yard in the hope of getting some information out of Sergeant Bird. Fortunately for him, Inspector Entwistle was out, and the sergeant was feeling disposed to talk, having conducted himself to advantage in the matter.

'He did his best to deny everything at first,' he said, when Freddy inquired as to whether they had made any progress in their questioning. 'Or, at least, he couldn't deny having a gun, because we found it on him, but he tried to bluster it out, and said he thought you were burglars—which in a manner of speaking you were,' he added pointedly.

Freddy affected an expression of boyish innocence that would not have fooled a child.

'Nothing of the sort, I assure you,' he said. 'Our motives were of the purest. What did he say about the cocaine?'

'He tried to pin the blame for that on you, too. Said you'd planted it on him. Lucky for you that your story about the shop on Commercial Street turned out to be true, isn't it? So you're off the hook there.'

'Splendid,' said Freddy dryly. 'Have you closed that place down, then?'

'Yes,' said Bird. 'We went in and caught quite a few of them red-handed. None of them will talk, of course, so we can't prove a link between them and the Kibbles, but as soon as we told Basil he'd been seen picking the stuff up outside the theatre he crumpled and admitted everything.'

'What about the packet from the Maypole? Did he admit to planting that?'

'Not in so many words, but he looked guilty enough when we mentioned it, and muttered something or other about having panicked at the sight of the police. However, he denies absolutely that he had anything to do with the cocaine we found in Miss Dacres' suite.'

'Really? You don't believe him, do you? She must have got it from him, surely.'

'Not to listen to him. As far as he's concerned, she was straight. But I suppose you'd expect him to say that if he thinks there's a murder charge in it for him.'

'Did he go out on the terrace at all during the fatal period?'

'As a matter of fact, it seems he did,' said the sergeant, looking pleased with himself. 'And he admits to speaking to Dorothy Dacres, too.'

'Does he, now?' said Freddy with sudden interest. 'Wherefore this sudden admission?'

The sergeant coughed.

'We—er—may have hinted that he'd been seen,' he said.

'And was he?'

'Perhaps he was,' said Bird. 'We'll come to that in a moment. Of course we suggested it just to get a confession out of him. After all, if he was the murderer then it stands to reason that he must have been out on the terrace with her at some point, so we needed him to admit it. He denied it at first, but we pointed out that if he made a clean breast of it, then he'd be more likely to make a favourable impression on the judge.'

'I see. At what time did he speak to Dorothy?'

'Just before eleven, he says. He went out for a breath of fresh air, but nobody saw him because he went through Miss Drucker's bedroom rather than out through the living-room doors, and stood on that side of the terrace, out of view. According to his story, he found Dorothy standing there, and passed the time of day with her for ten minutes or so. It was a perfectly ordinary conversation, and had nothing to do with drugs, since he swears she wasn't one of his clients, and that he barely knew her.'

'Do you believe him?'

Bird shrugged.

'He protested hard enough about it, but then people do when they're facing a prison sentence or worse,' he said.

'What did they talk about, if not drugs?' said Freddy.

'The party, mostly, it seems. But here's an interesting thing,' said the sergeant. 'Kibble claims Dacres told him she was waiting for someone.'

'She didn't say who, I take it?'

'No. She just said she'd been told to wait there, and wished they'd hurry up, because she was getting pretty cold.'

'She'd been *told* to wait there?' said Freddy thoughtfully.

'That's what Kibble said. Then she told him he'd better get back inside or he'd miss all the fun, so he went.'

'I see,' said Freddy. 'Then if his story is true, presumably the person she was waiting for was the person who killed her.'

'*If* it's true,' said Bird. 'And that brings us back to the question of whether he was seen with Dorothy or not.'

'Oh?'

'Yes. He says he was sure he heard a muffled sneeze nearby while they were talking, and had the strong impression that someone was listening to their conversation.'

'Curiouser and curiouser,' said Freddy. 'First of all we had no-one who would admit to having talked to Dorothy after she went missing, and now we have possibly two people.'

'I shouldn't set too much store by what Kibble says if I were you,' said Bird. 'I think we'll find he killed her, all right. The only difficulty will be in proving it. I can't see a jury convicting him on this sort of flimsy evidence.'

'True,' said Freddy. 'But since he's admitted to speaking to Dorothy, then why should he lie about the sneeze?'

'To shift the blame away from himself, I expect.'

'I suppose so. Still, if Basil's telling the truth about having spoken to her, we know now that Dorothy Dacres was still alive after eleven o'clock. And even if Basil *didn't* kill Dorothy, we also know that Robert Kenrick didn't do it either.'

'Oh? Why's that?'

'Because after Kenrick came in from the terrace at a little past eleven, he and Seymour Cosgrove went into the maid's room with a bottle of whisky,' said Freddy. 'That's according to Cosgrove, at any rate. And Gussie—Augusta Laing—is let out, too. She was out on the landing until just before eleven with Seymour, and then after that she was with me.'

'Ah,' said Bird, and made a note. 'That clears a few things up. But I don't think it makes much difference in the end, as I'm pretty sure we've got our man.'

'I expect you're right,' said Freddy doubtfully. 'I say, I don't suppose you happen to have a list of everybody's alibis, do you? Not for publication, naturally; I should just like to take a look at them, in case something strikes me. I mean to say, I was there anyway, so saw most of what was happening, but I don't know exactly what everyone was doing and at what time.'

'I don't see why not,' said Bird after a moment. He hunted through a pile of papers and pushed one across to Freddy. 'You can copy that down if you like. But don't tell the inspector,' he added.

'I won't say a word,' promised Freddy, and scribbled down some notes quickly. Then he thanked the sergeant and took his leave. He was by no means as certain as Sergeant Bird that Basil Kibble had murdered Dorothy Dacres. For one thing, there seemed to be too little motive. It was easy to jump to the conclusion that a man who was already known to have been engaging in illicit activities had taken things one step further and resorted to murder, but why had he done it? There was no evidence at all that Dorothy had threatened Basil—or even that they had known one another particularly well. And although he had admitted supplying cocaine, Basil had said Dorothy was 'straight.' In that case, where had the drugs found in her room come from? Then there was Basil's story that Dorothy had been waiting for someone. She had been told to wait on the terrace, he said. But that was odd, too, because if Freddy had found out anything about Dorothy Dacres, it was that she did not like to be *told* to do anything. Why had she agreed to wait there, rather than inside? Who had she arranged to meet? And the story about the sneeze: was it true? If it was, then was the mysterious listener also Dorothy's killer? None of it made sense.

Still, at least they knew one thing now: Dorothy had still been alive after eleven o'clock. That let out Robert Kenrick and Seymour Cosgrove, if Kenrick backed up Seymour's story about where they had gone. Gussie he had never believed capable of murder, but it was a relief at any rate to know for certain that she had not done it. Who else was left? Assuming that none of the crowd of hangers-on at the party that night had done it—and he supposed the police had looked carefully into that possibility—then only a few people had any reason to want Dorothy Dacres out of the way. What had they all been doing after eleven o'clock? Freddy took out his notebook and began to count them off as he walked. First, Cora Drucker, the dead woman's sister: she could not have done it, for she had talked to one person after another from the time of the announcement until her sister's body was found, and had been in sight all the time. Then there was Eugene Penk. He had been on the other terrace with Kenneth Neale for some of the time, then had remained there for a few more minutes after Neale came back into the living-room. Might Penk have done it after he came off the terrace? It did not seem so, for as far as Freddy could recall, he had returned to the living-room and called loudly for a drink at the same time that the functionary from the hotel had come to report the finding of Dorothy's body in the street. This was confirmed by Sarah Rowland, who had been watching everybody that evening from her chair by the wall. Might Penk have crept out of Dorothy's room when Sarah was looking in a different direction? It was possible, but then he would have had to creep back in again afterwards without being seen, in order to appear in time to receive the news from the manager. It seemed unlikely, to say the least. What about Kenneth Neale, then? He and Penk gave one another an alibi until about eleven, after which he had stormed back into the living-room and gone to speak to his wife, who had attempted to soothe his ruffled temper. Patience Neale had not been parted from Ada—and in any case, Freddy did not think she had a strong enough motive. It seemed, then, that nobody had had the opportunity. Perhaps Basil Kibble *had* done it after all. Freddy thought back to the night in Kennington, and recalled the grim look on Basil's face as he pointed the gun at them. There was no doubt he was ruthless enough to kill. Perhaps Freddy was looking for complications where none existed.

He stopped suddenly and stared at the paper in front of him, for the thought that had eluded him yesterday at the Abingdon had just come back to him. Now, that was odd. Why was it significant? Did it have a bearing on the murder? Might that be what had happened in this case? He shook his head. No; it was a stupid idea—absurd, in fact. He put the thought out of his mind and walked on, trying to concentrate on Robert Kenrick's alibi. But the idea would not be quashed; it kept intruding itself into his head and demanding to be taken seriously, so he stopped again and considered it carefully.

'It couldn't be possible, could it?' he murmured to himself. 'It would have been far too risky, surely.'

He set himself to think, and as he did so he remembered something Adorable Ada had said too, and which he had disregarded at the time. But why had he thought of it? Was it connected to his first idea? He thought he saw how it might be. He raised his eyebrows and whistled under his breath. The theory was far-fetched enough, but he was beginning to have a glimmer of an idea as to how Dorothy might have died.

'I wonder if it could have worked,' he said to himself. 'And how can I find out?'

CHAPTER TWENTY-TWO

O N SATURDAY FREDDY was wanted at the paper in the morning, and so had no time to think about his idea. As he came out of the *Clarion* building, he saw the unwelcome sight of Corky Beckwith coming along the street towards him. It was too late to avoid him, so Freddy accepted his fate with resignation. Corky was as full of himself as ever.

'I take it you've seen the news,' he said. 'They've charged Kibble with the murder of Dorothy Dacres.'

'So I see,' said Freddy.

'I must say, it's all turned out rather well for me,' went on Corky. 'You know it was I who found them, don't you?'

'Are you sure of that?' said Freddy. 'The police never mentioned it.'

'Didn't they? Perhaps they were too embarrassed at having failed to catch the fugitives themselves. If you ask me, they've put on a poor show altogether in this case. I mean to say, who was it who did all the detective-work in the first place? Had it not been for me, they'd never have known Kibble had anything to do with the matter, and a dangerous criminal would still be at large. Of course, you helped a little,' he added generously. 'But I suppose you were too tired to continue the search after our adventure. I was determined to pursue the story to the bitter end, however, and track him down. I do believe I've run up expenses of fifty pounds just on train fares in the past week, but one had to follow up any lead that came in, however tenuous. If you'll believe it, I spent a day and a half on a mountain-side in Wales, after we received reports that Kibble had disguised himself as a shepherd and taken to living in a wooden hut with a herd of sheep. Dreadfully uncivilized country it is, too,' he said with a shudder. 'And the Welsh! They're short and belligerent to a man, and barely speak a word of English—or at least, not the sort of English you or I would understand. I thought I should never get out alive.'

'Yes, I can imagine they wouldn't appreciate your unique talents,' said Freddy. 'And how's the cocaine situation in the hill-farms of Wales, might I ask? The air's positively thick with the stuff, I expect.'

'That's another of your jokes, of course,' said Corky. 'I couldn't tell you the answer, because I got out as soon as I could and hurried back to London, as I was worried I might have missed the Kibbles. Then the *Herald* received a tip-off that they'd been seen in Dover, so I headed there post-haste and was just in time to see the arrest.'

'Then it wasn't you who found them at all,' said Freddy.

'Well, yes, the police got there first, but I was the first reporter to arrive on the scene. It all amounts to the same thing for my purposes. Nobody cares about the police arresting somebody—it looks far better in print to say I tracked them down myself.'

'I see,' said Freddy.

'Still, a job well done, don't you think? The two of them have been locked up, and our citizens can sleep soundly in their beds once again.'

'I'd like to believe it,' said Freddy. 'But I don't think Basil murdered anyone.'

'Oh, but you saw for yourself what a violent man he is. Why, he was perfectly prepared to shoot us both without a second thought. Just think what a dreadful calamity that would have been! Can you imagine how the world would have mourned my loss?'

'It wouldn't have mourned you for a second, fathead. You might have got a paragraph on page ten on a slack news day.'

'Nonsense. I'm the star man at the *Herald* these days. They're very appreciative of my work in exposing this plague of illicit drugs that is sweeping the country.'

Freddy regarded him thoughtfully.

'Sometimes I'm almost convinced that you really believe what you say,' he said. 'You really are the most revolting hypocrite, aren't you?'

'No more than anybody else in this business, including you,' said Corky, wholly unperturbed. 'We've all heard about some of the things you and your titled pals get up to. Why, that story of what you, Bagley and Viscount Delamere did the night you broke into the London Zoo was going the rounds of Fleet Street for months. You ought to count yourself lucky you weren't arrested. If you had been, it wouldn't have gone well for you, since that sort of thing is very much frowned upon by the man in the street.'

'At least I don't pretend to be better than I am,' said Freddy, after only the briefest of pauses. 'I've never published screeds of pontificating tripe about the horrors of cocaine, shortly before planting a load of the stuff on someone else just to get a good story. It was you who put the dope in Dorothy's room, wasn't it? The cocaine the police found on her dressing-table was of a lower quality than the stuff they got from Basil—and besides, he denied he'd had anything to do with it. And he was telling the truth, because you planted it, didn't you?'

'I didn't *plant* it,' said Corky airily. 'I left it there accidentally, if you must know.'

'What?' said Freddy.

'Well, it's the sort of thing that might have happened to anyone. I was in her room, minding my own business—'

'You mean searching through her things?'

'Perhaps I might have glanced into one or two drawers, yes, but that wasn't the main reason I went in. It's hard work being a waiter, you know, and I was tired, as I'd been up early that day, and feeling in need of a pick-me-up, so as soon as I got the chance I slipped in to do the business in private, since I didn't have enough to share. I hadn't been there more than a minute or two when I heard a noise from outside and got the most awful fright. I'd forgotten about the other terrace, and hadn't thought to look and see whether anyone was on it.'

'At what time was this?' said Freddy suddenly.

'I don't know,' said Corky. 'Just after eleven, perhaps.'

'You mean after I'd told you not to go rifling through any more drawers?'

'Yes, yes,' said Corky impatiently. 'Does it matter?'

'And what exactly did you hear?'

'I don't know. A sort of scraping sound. The noise of someone moving around, you know.'

'Who was it?'

'Nobody, as it happens. I went across to the terrace door and just peeped out through the curtains, but I couldn't see anyone. And then I tried the door but it was locked, so I realized I must have been mistaken. At any rate, I knew I was wanted back at work, so I went back into the living-room. It was only later I remembered I'd left my little box of tricks on the dressing-table, but I never got the opportunity to go back and retrieve it. Why are you so interested in this anyway?'

'Oh, I don't know. Perhaps because everyone now thinks Dorothy Dacres took dope thanks to you,' said Freddy.

'That was unintentional—and in any case, all's well that ends well, don't you agree? The story wouldn't have been nearly so neat if the coke hadn't been found in Dacres' room. Basil was the guilty one anyway, and all I did was help prove that.'

'But you didn't know he had anything to do with cocaine that night at the party.'

'No,' conceded Corky. 'But I knew *someone* did, and I was hoping to flush them out.'

'What drivel you do talk,' said Freddy. 'Look here, the police really ought to know about this. If the stuff wasn't Dorothy's then there's nothing to connect her to Basil Kibble, and no reason for him to have killed her.'

'Of course he killed her,' said Corky. 'He's a dangerous man.'

'Dangerous or not, he had no motive, and you can't just go and pin the blame on him like that.'

'If you think I'm going to walk into a police station and gaily admit the stuff was mine, then you're very much mistaken,' said Corky. 'What do you take me for?'

'I have a list somewhere,' said Freddy.

'Well, put the thought out of your mind. I have no intention of coming clean, and if you squeal on me I shall simply deny it. There's no proof it was mine, and if you go around shouting about it everyone will just think you're trying to do in a rival reporter.' Freddy opened his mouth to protest, and Corky went on in an avuncular manner, 'Freddy, Freddy, there's no need to worry your head about it. Some little things are not meant to be interfered with. It will all come out in the wash, you'll see. Now, I really must be going. There's been a nasty motor accident on Oxford Street and I don't want to miss the dead bodies. You will look out for my piece, won't you?'

And so saying, he went off with a cheery wink and a wave, leaving Freddy standing deep in thought.

CHAPTER TWENTY-THREE

I F WHAT CORKY had said was true, then it was starting to look as though Freddy's idea might not be as far-fetched as he had believed. What he really needed was to get back into Dorothy Dacres' suite at the Abingdon and have a good scout around. Or, on second thoughts, perhaps it would make more sense to call Scotland Yard and turn the matter over to them. Inspector Entwistle already considered him an interferer— and after all, catching murderers was the job of the police, not newspaper reporters. Perhaps he would telephone them and see what they thought of his idea. Accordingly, Freddy went back to the *Clarion*'s offices and made the call. Inspector Entwistle and Sergeant Bird were out, he was informed by a polite woman, but he was welcome to leave a message if he liked. Freddy gave a brief explanation of his theory. It sounded silly even as he said it, and the woman seemed surprised, but said she would tell the inspector as soon as he returned.

Jolliffe was sitting at his desk, and addressed him with a conspiratorial air when he put the telephone down.

'How are you getting on with the Dacres case?' he said. 'I see they've arrested Basil and Birdie. Now, there's a scandal. Who would have thought it? I mean to say, I shouldn't have thought they needed the money.'

'These people live from one job to the next,' said Freddy. 'And I don't think the Kibbles are quite the big thing they were a few years ago. Perhaps they were a little down on their luck. Besides, it seems that Birdie is addicted to the stuff, and it's an expensive habit, so I dare say that's how they got into it in the first place.'

'And it looks as though it led to murder,' said Jolliffe. 'Funny—if you'd asked me, I'd have guessed the motive was something to do with money, not drugs.'

'There's no saying it wasn't,' said Freddy. 'I'm not convinced that Basil Kibble did it.'

'No?'

'No. Tell me your idea about the money.'

'Well, I don't exactly know,' said Jolliffe, considering. 'It's just that the presence of Dorothy Dacres prevented one or two people from doing very well for themselves—or should I say, rather, the presence of Henry Aston, since I understand he was pushing for her to be given a contract that would guarantee her the lead rôle in Aston-Penk's next three pictures.' He leaned forward. 'Keep it on the q.t, but I hear that far from being philosophical about giving Dorothy the part of Helen Harper, Eugene Penk was actually tearing his hair out over it.'

'Oh?' said Freddy.

'Yes. You might think all these film types were rolling in it, but as a matter of fact Penk is a bit short of the ready. The money he put into Aston-Penk was all borrowed, you see, and the banks have been starting to ask for a return. The company is Penk's baby, and for all his talking-up of Henry Aston, he regrets having gone into business with him, because he keeps trying to interfere with the artistic side of things.'

'Yes, I'd heard something about that,' said Freddy.

'The banks were pressing hard, and it was starting to look as though Penk would have to ask Aston for more money—which would have given Aston even more power. Penk wanted the money, but didn't want the conditions attached to it.'

'Those conditions being Dorothy Dacres.'

'Exactly. But as luck would have it, Sir Aldridge agreed to step in with some funds.'

'That happened after Dorothy died, didn't it?' said Freddy, thinking.

'Yes,' said Jolliffe.

'And I expect old Feathers hadn't been keen on having an American play the lead in *For Every Yesterday*?'

'He certainly wanted to present the film as an English production, at any rate,' said Jolliffe.

'Another reason to put Dorothy out of the way,' said Freddy. 'Henry Aston wanted her but Sir Aldridge didn't. Why was Aston so wild about her, anyway? Were they having an affair?'

'I don't think so—at least, not as far as I know—but he did have a kind of obsession with her. She knew it, of course, and took advantage of it.'

'I wonder why she and Penk never divorced,' said Freddy. 'I mean to say, they'd kept the marriage a secret for years anyway. Why not end it without a fuss?'

'She knew which side her bread was buttered on, I imagine,' said Jolliffe. 'As long as they were still married she knew she retained some influence in Hollywood. She wasn't getting any younger, you know, and as long as she stayed on good terms with Penk, there was always the hope that he would help her find parts.'

'I wonder whether she wasn't playing dog in the manger,' said Freddy. 'I saw them all yesterday, and Dorothy's sister and Penk were looking pretty cosy together. I shouldn't be a bit surprised if Dorothy suspected something of that sort and held it over their heads out of spite.'

'If you say so. I don't know anything about it.'

'Whatever the case, Dorothy's death must have come as something of a relief to Penk,' said Freddy.

'I gather he has an alibi, though,' said Jolliffe significantly.

'He does at the moment,' said Freddy. 'But as it happens, I've had a little idea about how to break it.'

'You think he did it, then?'

'I don't know, but I should very much like to find out. I can believe in his guilt far more than Basil's.'

'If Penk did do it, then that will put paid to the film altogether,' observed Jolliffe. 'And after all the fuss that's been made over it.'

'True, but that can't be helped. I know everyone thinks Dorothy wasn't right for the part, but there are politer ways of turning a woman down than by throwing her off a building.'

'Oh, undoubtedly,' said Jolliffe.

'Perhaps someone else will make the film,' said Freddy. 'Sir Aldridge, for example. After all, it's an English play, and it might turn out better without the interference of the Americans.'

'Very loud, Americans,' said Jolliffe. 'But rather handy at golf.'

He went back to his work, and Freddy wondered what to do next. He was impatient to hear from Scotland Yard, to find out what they thought of his theory, but it seemed they were in no hurry to return his call. At last the telephone rang, and he snatched up the receiver. It was Gussie.

'Come along to the Abingdon if you want an exclusive,' she said. 'They've decided to go ahead with the picture after all, and I'm to be Helen Harper. I'm having to pinch myself, as I can't quite believe it's real.'

Freddy offered his congratulations, and she giggled delightedly.

'Thank you. It's been an odd couple of weeks, to say the least, but I hope things will go smoothly now. We're in the top floor suite and Seymour is taking photos, so do come along, won't you?'

'All right,' said Freddy. 'I'll see you in half an hour, but you'd better tell Seymour to keep his hands to himself.'

'Don't worry, he won't hit you again,' said Gussie.

'I was talking about you, not me,' said Freddy.

'Oh, yes, I'm sorry about the other day,' she said. 'Terribly bad form, wasn't it? But you forgive us, don't you? He does love me so, and I'm simply crazy about him.'

Freddy assured her that he had not taken offence, and she giggled again and hung up.

This was the opportunity Freddy had been waiting for. He instructed Jolliffe to tell the police where he had gone if they called, and left the office.

CHAPTER TWENTY-FOUR

WHEN FREDDY ARRIVED at the top floor suite of the Abingdon—the penthouse which had once been that of Dorothy Dacres—he found the place full of people and in a state of confusion. The first thing he saw was Seymour Cosgrove, who was striding about, arranging pieces of photographic equipment and snapping at anyone who got in his way. Gussie and Robert Kenrick were sitting on a sofa in close conversation, while Kenneth Neale, looking uncomfortable in a smart suit, submitted to the ministrations of his wife, who was attempting to tame his sparse hair with a comb.

'These Americans set great store by the way one looks,' she was saying. 'One might be the most talented director in the world, but they won't care about that if one's tailoring is wrong.'

'But I won't be wearing this sort of thing on the set, my dear,' said Neale. 'I much prefer to be comfortable.'

'No matter, when this is the photograph that will appear in all the press. There,' she said, stepping back to regard her handiwork. 'You look quite distinguished. I see I shall have to keep an eye on you when we get to America. The Hollywood studios are full of pretty young ladies, I understand.'

'None so pretty as you, my sweet,' he said, and they beamed fondly at one another.

Elsewhere in the room, Cora Drucker was in conversation with a middle-aged woman who, Freddy was soon given to understand, was to play the part of the maid which had originally been given to Birdie Kibble. Meanwhile, Ada Neale sat rigidly in a chair, watching proceedings and occasionally smoothing the folds of her pink satin dress.

'Hallo,' she said when she saw Freddy. 'Have you come to see me having my photograph taken?'

'I suppose I have,' he replied. 'Are you looking forward to the film?'

'Yes,' she said. 'I think I shall like it now. I wasn't very excited about it when I thought I should have to work with Dorothy, but I like Augusta. She's very pretty, isn't she?'

'Oh, certainly,' said Freddy, and indeed Gussie was looking radiant that day. She was dressed in a pale blue evening-gown that suited her complexion perfectly, while her hair was brushed and gleaming, and looked more than ever like a fiery halo against her pale skin. At that moment she caught sight of Freddy, and jumped up to greet him.

'I'm so glad you've come,' she said in a low voice. 'I know one oughtn't to crow, but I can't help feeling triumphant at last. It's awful of me, isn't it?'

'Life goes on,' said Freddy.

'Yes, it does,' she said with a determined lift of the chin.

Eugene Penk came in just then, saw Freddy and gave him a nod, then went to talk to a man who had been standing at the side of the room in self-effacing fashion, watching proceedings.

'That's Oscar Hoffman,' said Gussie. 'He's Henry Aston's right-hand man, and he's been sent over to keep an eye on things.'

'Things?'

'The money, I think. I gather it was touch and go as to whether Aston would withdraw after Dorothy died, but Eugene managed to persuade him the venture was sound. But he's sent Mr. Hoffman over all the same, to make certain everything is as it should be.'

'You mean to make certain nobody else dies unexpectedly?' said Freddy.

Gussie gave him a look of alarm.

'Oh, goodness,' she said. 'Let's hope nothing like that happens. I don't think anybody's nerves could stand it.'

Seymour was now ready to begin shooting.

'Gussie, you come over here and stand by the piano,' he said. 'We'll have Kenrick in a moment, too.'

Gussie did as she was asked. Cora gave an exclamation and put her hand to her mouth.

'Oh!' she cried. 'Dorothy! Don't you remember, Seymour? She stood there too, just like that, in a dress the same colour.'

There was a little silence as everybody stared at Gussie, who looked down at her frock in dismay.

'I'm so terribly sorry, Cora,' she said. 'I didn't know. Should you like me to change it? I can send for another, if you like.'

'No,' said Cora. 'It's all right. It was just that, for a moment, I thought—'

She stopped, and Seymour broke in impatiently.

'I won't let you change,' he said. 'That one is perfect. Now, let's start.'

He began to take pictures, and everyone gathered around to watch. Freddy made conversation with a group of film people he had never met before, then drifted away and towards the door to Dorothy Dacres' old bedroom. Nobody was looking, so he opened the door quietly and went in. Signs of habitation indicated that someone else was staying in this room now— presumably Cora, Freddy thought. A dress had been thrown across a chair, and there were one or two bottles of scent on the dressing-table. The room was dim, for the heavy curtains were pulled almost closed across the double door to the second terrace, which was bolted from the inside. Freddy unbolted it and passed through. This terrace was much smaller than the main one—little more than a balcony, really—and gave out onto the street on which the hotel's front entrance was located. While the big terrace was intended for large summer parties, this one was private and sheltered, with a little table and chairs for anyone who wished to breakfast outside. Here it was clear to see that the penthouse was at the very top of the building, for the terrace was formed from a sort of square recess cut out of the roof, which sloped upwards to his right and left. Freddy went across to the iron railing and stared down into the street. He was very high up. Then he turned and looked back at the building. Here, near the railing, the side wall was little more than waist high, and it would be a matter of seconds to jump up onto the sloping part of the roof. But first there was the question of the locked door which Corky had mentioned. How had Penk shut himself out here so his absence would not be discovered? Freddy's eye fell on a broom standing in the corner next to the door, and he went across to pick it up. He pushed the double doors closed and slid the handle of the broom through the two door handles. It was a very tight fit, and when he attempted to pull the doors open, they barely moved. That seemed to answer that question, he thought.

Freddy returned to the wall by the railing and pulled himself up onto the roof. It was very easy. There had been a frost that morning and the roof tiles were damp and slippery in places, but Freddy held on to the vertical part of the terrace wall for balance and was soon on top of the building. This part of the roof was flat, and from here it took only seconds to run quietly across and look down over a decorative parapet onto the main terrace. Below was the area that led out from the living-room. As he was peeping over the edge he heard voices, and moved back out of sight as the door opened and someone came out.

'It's a glorious day,' came Patience Neale's voice below. 'Is the sun too low in the sky to get a picture out here, do you suppose?'

Freddy moved along behind the parapet and looked down onto the section of terrace outside Cora's old room, which was out of sight of the other area. According to Basil Kibble, this was where Dorothy had been standing on the night she died, waiting for someone. If Freddy's theory was correct, Eugene Penk had crept across here that night. Had he crouched behind the parapet and watched from the same spot on which Freddy was now standing, awaiting the right moment? Freddy could see it in his mind's eye: Dorothy, shivering in her thin evening-gown, talking to Basil Kibble, who had nipped outside for some fresh air. Basil had heard a muffled sneeze, he said—presumably Penk, as he waited for Basil to go indoors. Then what had happened after that? Penk must have swung himself down over the parapet—an easy enough task for a man who had been both a sportsman and a stunt-man in his time—then, perhaps before Dorothy had even seen him or had time to speak, had, in one swift, ruthless movement, picked her up and thrown her over the edge. Freddy suddenly remembered standing on the other side of the terrace that night and hearing a shriek of what he had thought was laughter. Had it been laughter? Or had it in fact been a scream of terror from Dorothy Dacres as she plummeted to her doom?

Freddy cast his eyes about. It would have been simple enough for Penk to jump down onto the terrace from here, but how had he got back up again? The answer was there below him. The table and chairs he had examined on the night of the party were standing next to an ornamental pillar. To hoist himself up from the table to the top of the pillar and thence to the roof would have been reasonably easy for a man in good condition. Freddy made a mental note to try and get a look at the shoes Penk had been wearing that evening, since there was a good chance they would have been scraped in the climb—indeed, he could see one or two streaks on the parapet that might perhaps have been shoe-leather, although could the traces still be there after all this time?

He was starting to think he had been up here long enough, for his absence would surely be noticed soon. He went along to the other side of the terrace one last time, to try and judge how risky the venture would have been, given that several people—Freddy included—had been outside at the very moment Dorothy had been thrown over the railing, and saw that more members of the party had now come outside. Adorable Ada was standing by the railing, practising her smiles, as Seymour moved about, seeking the best angle from which to photograph her. Kenneth Neale and Eugene Penk looked out over the rooftops and murmured together, while Gussie lounged in a chair, smoking a cigarette and exchanging the occasional flirtatious glance with Seymour. Freddy was just about to turn away and return over the roof to the other terrace, when his foot knocked against a loose stone. Quickly he moved back, but it was too late, for Ada had looked up and seen him.

'What are you doing up there?' she said in surprise.

Everyone turned and stared, including Penk, who went very still for an instant but said nothing.

Freddy sat on the parapet and tried to look as though he had merely gone up there to enjoy the sunshine, and that sitting on roofs was quite a regular habit of his.

'I say, there's a splendid view from here,' he said.

'Come down from there, you idiot,' said Gussie. 'You'll fall.'

Freddy hesitated, for he had just remembered that he had barred the door to the other terrace, and if he came down onto the main terrace then they would have to break it down to get outside again.

'Just a second,' he said. He ran back across the roof and made his way back carefully down to Dorothy's balcony. He pulled the broom out from between the door handles with difficulty and opened the door, and at that very moment realized his mistake, as Eugene Penk stepped outside.

CHAPTER TWENTY-FIVE

F REDDY TOOK A step back.

'What were you doing up there?' said Penk.

He picked up the broom and barred the door again. Although he must have been twice Freddy's age and more, Freddy now saw how strong he looked, and did not much fancy his chances against him. Penk's shoulders were wide and powerful, and he had the forearms of the boxer he had once been. Freddy knew he was trapped now, and decided he might as well make the most of it.

'I was testing a theory,' he said.

'Oh?'

'Yes. I wanted to know whether I could see the Houses of Parliament from the roof. But in the end I got distracted and forgot to look. Perhaps you know the answer. Can you see them?'

'Why are you asking me that? How should I know?'

'No, I suppose you wouldn't,' said Freddy. 'It was dark, wasn't it?'

Penk regarded him without speaking for a moment.

'I don't know what you're talking about,' he said at last.

'I think you do,' said Freddy. 'I think you're very familiar with the route from this balcony to the terrace on the other side of the building.'

'Is that so?' said Penk. He had not taken his eyes off Freddy, and was staring at him much as a snake might stare at a mouse as it contemplated the best direction from which to strike.

Freddy continued, perhaps recklessly:

'That's how you did it, isn't it? Killed your wife, I mean. Or perhaps you didn't consider her your wife any more. After all, you'd been separated for long enough. But after all this time she was starting to become—what do they call it? A millstone around your neck. She was too demanding, and her demands were threatening the future of Aston-Penk and all the hard work you'd put into it to build it up. Henry Aston had got a sort of *idée fixe* about her, and was insisting on putting her in all your pictures in future. It was he who wanted her for the part of Helen Harper. But you knew she was no good for the rôle—just as everybody else knew it. Kenneth Neale didn't want her, and wouldn't have joined the film had he known she was going to get the part. You got him under false pretences and thought you'd be able to talk him round, but he was threatening lawyers. It was dreadfully important to you that this film did not fail. You were running out of money, and the only person you could go to for it was the very man who was unwittingly sabotaging the company by insisting on interfering. You spoke to Sir Aldridge about the possibility of his putting money into the venture, and thought he might agree, but he was keen on keeping the film British through and through, and Dorothy was an obstacle to that.'

'Clever, aren't you?' said Penk.

'On top of that, there was the question of Cora,' went on Freddy. 'I saw the two of you together the other day, and it was obvious there was something going on. Was Dorothy standing in the way of you both?'

'Dorothy never could bear anyone to have anything of hers,' said Penk. 'Especially not Cora. She was a child in many respects. She'd had things all her own way for so long that she never learned how to share or play nice.'

'So I understand,' said Freddy.

He was eyeing the door, wondering whether he might take Penk by surprise and make a run at it. But the broom fitted stiffly through the door handles, and he knew he was unlikely to succeed. All he could do was to try and keep Penk talking until someone realized the two of them were missing, since he was very aware that behind him was a precipitous drop of six storeys. He went on:

'At any rate, you wanted rid of her, so you took matters into your own hands. I don't know how long you'd been planning it, but I'm sure you were watching events closely that evening in case the opportunity should arise—as it did. You encouraged Kenneth Neale to follow you onto the terrace here, and made sure you were both seen going that way. You talked, and then said something to calm him down and sent him back into the living-room, while you stayed here. This was to be your alibi, and you didn't want someone coming out and finding you weren't here, so you jammed the door shut and then climbed up onto the roof. You went across and saw Dorothy standing outside Cora's room talking to Basil, and waited until he'd gone back indoors. Then you jumped down, threw her over the edge and hared back the way you had come. A few minutes later you made a great show of coming out into the living-room and calling for a drink, just as the manager of the hotel arrived to tell you that Dorothy had been found dead. It was a good alibi, but as you can see, I've just shown everyone how it can be broken. I should never have thought of it had I not been forced to scramble across a roof myself a few days ago. It's just unlucky for you that it gave me the idea as to how you might have done it.'

Penk gave a short laugh.

'I always knew you reporters were full of invention,' he said. 'Try getting that one past the police. They'll never believe it. Where's the proof?'

Freddy put his hand into his pocket and brought something out.

'I found this up on the roof just now,' he said. 'It's a button. It looks as though it's fallen from an evening-suit. Have you examined yours lately? Any buttons missing?'

For the first time an expression of uncertainty passed across Penk's face.

'I shall give this to the police later,' said Freddy. 'Let's see what they make of it. And now, if you don't mind, I'd like to go in. It's getting a little chilly out here.'

'You don't think I'm going to let you back in, do you?' said Penk. He moved slowly across towards Freddy, who was standing by the railing. Freddy glanced at the door with the broom handle shoved through it and made a dart for it, but Penk blocked his way. Slowly he advanced, driving Freddy back towards the railing. But Freddy had no intention of going without a fight. He stumbled, as though he had tripped over his own feet, and fell against the side wall. Penk hesitated just for a second, and in that second Freddy scrambled around him and back towards the door on his hands and knees. It had been a clumsy move, and it failed; Penk grabbed him by the collar and hauled him to his feet, but before he could get hold of Freddy's arm, Freddy had wrenched himself free and made a dive for the terrace wall. In a trice he was up and climbing towards the flat part of the roof. If he could make it as far as there, he would surely be safe, since he was much younger and faster than Penk, and could run across and jump down onto the other terrace. But the roof tiles were still slippery, causing him to lose his footing several times, and he had barely reached the top when Penk caught up with him and brought him down. It was now that Freddy found out how physically powerful the other man was, as he felt a pair of strong hands around his neck, beginning to throttle him. Freddy flailed uselessly for a second, then remembered the fight with Seymour at the Maypole and, bringing his arm up, poked his fingers hard into Penk's eyes. Penk growled in pain and loosened his hold, and Freddy immediately leapt up and made another bolt for it, giving a loud yell as he did so. He was hoping to bring someone to his aid, although he knew it was a forlorn hope, since who would be likely to climb up onto the roof after them? At any rate, he thought that someone might realize what was going on and call the police. He reached the parapet of the main terrace just as Penk caught up with him and seized him by the neck from behind. If Freddy had been hoping for help there he was disappointed, for everyone had gone in now. He was just in time to see Seymour carrying the last of his things back through the door to the living-room, his face set in its usual scowl, before Penk dragged him away from the parapet. Freddy gave a strangled shout but Seymour did not look up.

'Shut up, will you?' said Penk through gritted teeth.

He now had Freddy in a head-lock and was dragging him across to another part of the roof which sloped down steeply, with no protection, straight to the street. It was clear he intended to hurl Freddy over the edge.

'You can't do this,' panted Freddy as he tried to wrestle himself free. 'Nobody will believe it was an accident.'

'Yes they will,' said Penk. 'Everybody saw you up here before. It'll just look like you slipped. They'll call it a tragic coincidence. Now, keep still, won't you?'

He jerked Freddy forward as he spoke. Freddy could hardly breathe, but with a little struggle managed to turn his head towards Penk and free up his air-way. With his left arm he reached up behind Penk's shoulder, then made a grab for his nose and twisted it hard, at the same time jerking Penk's head suddenly backwards as far as it would go. With a roar of pain Penk released Freddy's neck, and the two of them overbalanced and fell over. Now Penk was in a rage. He swung a fist at Freddy's face, but Freddy rolled out of the way just in time. The two men grappled on the ground, Freddy attempting to poke Penk in the eye again, for he knew he had no chance of beating him in a fist-fight. But Penk was now wise to Freddy's methods; he jabbed a knee into Freddy's stomach, winding him, then, still pinning him down with the knee, held his wrists with one hand and cuffed him across the head with the other. He was wearing a heavy gold ring which caught Freddy above the eye, leaving a deep cut that began to bleed.

Then Penk got to his feet and began dragging Freddy with grim determination across the roof towards the edge. There seemed no escape, and Freddy began to consider whether a short prayer might be appropriate in the circumstances. A passing rag-and-bone cart with an old mattress on it would do nicely. Or perhaps he might catch hold of the gutter as he slid over the edge, and cling onto that until help arrived. He kicked with all his might, but his wrists were pinned with a grip of iron. At last they reached the edge, and Penk jerked Freddy upright and prepared to give him a shove, but Freddy took his chance and kicked Penk's leg out from under him. Down they both went again, this time dangerously close to the edge of the roof. Freddy's head was dangling downwards into thin air; he could feel blood running into his hair, and he was beginning to feel a little dizzy, as Penk gripped his shoulders and did his best to push him further over. This was the end, surely. Freddy shut his eyes, but just as he was about to give it all up as lost, he thought he heard a shout, and felt Penk loosen his hold. Quick as a flash he opened his eyes again and rolled away from the edge. Through a haze of blood he saw figures running across the roof towards them. Penk was standing by the edge, bent almost double, breathing heavily and clutching at his chest.

'My heart!' he wheezed. He had gone blue about the lips and was beginning to sway. As Freddy sat up and wiped the blood from his eyes, he saw Penk totter gently, then sag to his knees and fall sideways. For one dreadful second the top half of his unconscious form hung, motionless, across the edge of the roof, then gravity took effect and the rest of his body followed. It slid down the steeply sloping roof, gathering speed as it went, and then disappeared into the abyss. Freddy winced and looked away. There was a short silence.

'Are you all right, sir?' came a familiar voice. Freddy looked up and saw Sergeant Bird and a young constable standing at a cautious distance from the edge of the roof. The constable looked a little green in the face, and as though he had much rather not be there.

'Ask me tomorrow,' said Freddy weakly.

'We'll get you inside when you've got your breath back,' said Bird. 'Johnson, go and tell the inspector he'd better close the street off outside. Let's just hope Mr. Penk didn't land on anybody.'

The constable went off. Freddy dragged himself a little further away from the edge and got carefully to his feet, and as he did so, he saw Seymour Cosgrove standing there in front of him, holding a camera.

'Got it all here,' said Seymour. 'That ought to make a bit of a splash for you in your paper tomorrow.'

He flashed a brief grin. Freddy stared at him.

'Yes, I expect it will,' he said at last.

CHAPTER TWENTY-SIX

TWO DAYS LATER Freddy returned to the Abingdon Hotel, at the behest of Cora Drucker, who wanted to speak to him. He waited for her in the lounge, thankful to remain firmly on the ground floor this time—not that he expected a repeat of the other day's events, but it was better to be safe than sorry. When she arrived she was dressed in tasteful black, and looked pale but composed.

'Oh, I expect I'll get by,' she said in reply to his inquiries as to her well-being. 'I won't deny it's been a shock, but I'm trying to look on the bright side of things. I was very fond of him and all—at least, I thought I was. He wanted to marry me, and he said he didn't care that I wasn't in love with him, but would be content with my friendship, if that was all I could give him. I'd almost made up my mind to say yes when it all came to an end the other day. I had no idea he was so wicked.'

She fished in her pocket for a handkerchief and dabbed it to her eyes.

'I guess I had a lucky escape,' she said after a minute. 'I ought to look at it that way, oughtn't I? He killed Dorothy because she got in his way, and he might have done the same to me one day. What if he decided I was too much trouble to him? I should never have been safe.'

'I suppose not,' said Freddy.

'But listen to me, talking about myself,' she said with a little laugh. 'I really wanted to ask how you are, since you're the one who nearly got killed.'

'Oh, I'm as right as rain,' said Freddy. 'Nothing wrong with me, apart from a few bruises and this little cut above the eye. In a day or two I shall have forgotten the whole thing.'

'It was lucky for you the police arrived when they did,' she said.

'Yes, it was,' he said. 'As it happened, I'd left a message at Scotland Yard, and they wanted to speak to Penk anyway, so turned up at the hotel just in time. And fortunately, Seymour had seen us on the roof and thought something was up, so they knew where to find us.'

'It's a good thing you found that button,' she said. 'Without that, there would have been no proof.'

Freddy considered admitting that he had mentioned the button to Penk on the spur of the moment, and that it had actually fallen from his own jacket some days earlier, but decided against it, for it could make no difference now. There was no doubt that Penk had been the murderer, but as Cora said, there had been no evidence of that, and the button had been the only way Freddy could think of to provoke Penk into action, so he said nothing.

'Well, I'm very glad you're all right,' said Cora. 'And I have Eugene to thank for one thing, at least.'

'Oh?'

'Yes. A few days before this all happened, he set up a meeting for me with one of the big studios back in Hollywood. If I can impress them then maybe they'll give me a contract. It's a great opportunity for me. Acting is the only thing I've ever wanted to do, and now I've been given a second chance to make a success of it.'

'A Hollywood studio, eh? But not Aston-Penk. I suppose that's no more?'

'I don't know about that,' said Cora. 'The men are talking about it—Henry Aston and Sir Aldridge Featherstone, I mean. But Eugene was the creative force behind the venture, so I don't know whether the company can continue. As a matter of fact, that's part of the reason I asked you to come. You work for Sir Aldridge, and I wondered whether you knew anything about it. I thought that if they were keeping the company open, and were still planning to make *For Every Yesterday*, then they might be looking for someone to fill Augusta's old part, since I guess she'll be playing Helen Harper now.'

'And you'd like to put yourself forward for the rôle, eh?'

Something in his tone must have put her on the alert, for she glanced up sharply. His face revealed nothing, however.

'Well, I don't see why not,' she said. 'One has to start somewhere. I suppose you think I'm hard-hearted, taking care of my own concerns only a couple of weeks after Dorothy died. But life goes on, and I know she'd hate to think of me sitting and moping over all this. I've lost my sister and the man I wanted to marry. I'm alone in the world now, and I have to look after myself.'

'You do indeed,' said Freddy. 'And I expect you'll do it very well, since from what I've seen of you, I should say you're an even better actress than your sister was.'

'What do you mean?' she said.

'Why, that you're putting on a very good show now—so good that I should almost believe it if I didn't know better.'

'I don't know what you're talking about,' she said, disconcerted. 'What show do you mean?'

'Well, I don't know what the casting chaps would call it, but I should call this part you're playing now "The Brave Bereaved," and it will certainly convince most people.'

'That's rather rude,' she said after a moment.

'Then there was the one you played on the night your sister died,' went on Freddy deliberately. 'I should say that's best described as "The Cunning Accomplice."'

She said nothing, and he continued:

'I'd always wondered what Dorothy was doing on the terrace that night. It was cold out there, and she had a roomful of devoted admirers ready to hang upon her every word inside. We all thought she must have gone out for just a few moments, perhaps for some fresh air, or to talk to someone, but that doesn't quite fit in with how the murder was done, does it? I mean to say, Penk was hardly going to bother running about on the rooftops just on the off-chance he might find her standing on the terrace by herself. He must have known she'd be there if his plan was to work. And then Basil Kibble said something odd, too: he talked to Dorothy on the terrace that night, just before she died. According to him, Dorothy said she'd been *told* to wait there. Now, I didn't know Dorothy well, but one thing I do know is that she didn't take kindly to being told what to do. She liked to be the one in charge. I wondered about it then, but in the end disregarded it, as I assumed Basil must have expressed himself badly. But then when we were all here the other day having tea, that little girl Ada Neale said something rather interesting. I was only half-listening so I almost missed it, but afterwards I remembered it and started thinking. Ada said that she should like to have a sister, because a sister would arrange surprises for her, as you did for Dorothy. As I said, I wasn't really listening at the time, but later the remark came back to me, and so I telephoned Patience Neale and asked to speak to Ada. She said she'd seen you take Dorothy to one side at the party, and had overheard you tell her to go into your room and wait outside on the terrace, as there was to be a surprise. She was to stand there out of the way, and pretend she knew nothing about it until it was ready. You said you'd come and fetch her when it was time. When I heard that, Basil's claim that Dorothy had been told to wait outside made perfect sense. If Dorothy thought she was going to receive a big surprise and be the centre of attention again, then of course she would do whatever she was told.'

Cora opened her mouth as though to speak, but thought better of it, and Freddy continued:

'A little after that, you were seen by Sarah Rowland going into Dorothy's room. I imagine you just glanced through the door at Penk and Kenneth Neale on the balcony, to give Penk the signal that Dorothy was now waiting on the other terrace and that he was to get rid of Neale. Then you went back into the living-room. You'd already been running around, talking to people and apparently looking for Robert Kenrick—I expect just to draw attention to yourself and establish an alibi, so that people would remember what you had been doing. As it happened, Kenrick was out on the main terrace, and you went out and tried to persuade him to go in. It was very important that you keep people away from the terrace—or, at least, that part of it outside your room, and so you kept him talking for as long as you could, while at the same time keeping an eye out for anyone else who might take it into their heads to venture outside. Then Gussie and I came out and Kenrick went back inside, while you made sure you stayed with us and stopped us going round to the other side of the terrace. I remember hearing a cry at the time, but thought it was someone laughing. I don't suppose you heard it, did you? That was the sound of your sister being thrown to her death.'

A tear rolled down Cora Drucker's face, and she began to twist her handkerchief in her hands.

'It was all arranged between you and Penk, wasn't it?' said Freddy. 'I shall give you the benefit of the doubt and assume the plan was all his own work. I imagine he'd had the idea some time earlier while he was out on the smaller terrace. He must have noticed, just as I did, how easy it would be to get up onto the roof from there, and what an excellent alibi his presence there would make, since the only way to get from the small terrace to the large one was apparently to come through Dorothy's bedroom and the living-room. I expect he did a dummy run beforehand, too, to make quite certain he could pull it off.

But he couldn't carry out his plan alone. He needed someone to help him, and that person was you. Your job was to get Dorothy onto the terrace, then keep everyone else away from it while Penk did the deed. I suppose you were both hoping it would be put down to an accident—but if it wasn't, then there would be plenty of witnesses to say that neither of you could have done it.'

'I didn't know what he was planning, I swear,' she burst out. 'It was he who told me there was to be a surprise, and that I was to get Dorothy out of the way. I thought maybe he'd arranged a big cake for her, or something, so I went along with it and told her to go and wait outside. Then it all happened and I still didn't understand that he'd done it—not until afterwards. He said he'd done it for us; that Dorothy had stood in everyone's way and would do nothing but make our lives a misery. He said I'd never be a star so long as she was alive, as she'd see to it that nobody would hire me, and he said Aston-Penk was in danger too, because Henry Aston was so infatuated with her that he was ruining everything. She'd done nothing to break the terms of her contract, either, so Eugene couldn't get rid of her that way. He'd had no choice, he said.' She glanced up at Freddy. 'I guess you can imagine how I felt when I found out I'd been an accomplice to my own sister's murder, but I swear to you I had no idea of it. I've been living in torment ever since that night. To go through each day, pretending I was as puzzled as everybody else about what happened, when I knew the man who'd done it was sitting right next to me—why, it's been almost unbearable. I've such a weight of guilt on my heart that I don't know whether I'll ever get over it. You do believe me, don't you? You do believe I'd never have done anything deliberately to hurt Dorothy? It was the most dreadful mistake, and now I shall have to live with it for the rest of my life.'

She gazed at him with a look of appeal. He returned her gaze appraisingly.

'It's a good story,' he said at last. 'I advise you to stick to it.'

Her brows drew together, and for just the briefest of moments her expression reminded him forcibly of the petulant frown he had seen on Dorothy Dacres' face on that very first day in the street outside the Abingdon.

'Then you *don't* believe me,' she said.

'You told me only a few minutes ago that you'd still been planning to marry Penk even after you knew what he'd done. Doesn't exactly square with your story, does it?' He held up his hand as she opened her mouth to say something, and went on, 'You're right—I don't believe you. But what does it matter what I believe? Nothing will ever be proved. There's no evidence, so you can deny it all you like and nobody will ever be able to say your involvement was anything other than unwitting. You're quite safe. Besides, your conscience is none of my business. You're the one who has to live with it.'

He stood up.

'Goodbye, Miss Drucker,' he said. 'I look forward to seeing you in your first starring rôle.'

She did not offer to shake hands, but sat and watched him as he left the lounge. When he looked back she was still gazing after him, her face expressionless.

Chapter Twenty-seven

A LTHOUGH FREDDY WAS right in saying that there was no proof Cora Drucker's involvement in her sister's murder had been deliberate, he decided to mention it to the police in any case. Inspector Entwistle and Sergeant Bird listened to his tale with interest.

'Cora Drucker, eh?' said the inspector thoughtfully. 'Yes, it makes sense. Either Penk was tremendously lucky—which doesn't seem likely—or someone must have been there to make sure he wasn't disturbed. You're right, of course: we'll never prove it, but I suppose there's no harm in going along there and questioning her, just to let her know we've got our eye on her.'

'You'll have to be quick, as she's returning to the States tomorrow,' said Freddy.

'There's probably just time to do it before lunch,' said Entwistle. 'The super wants to see me now, but if he doesn't keep me too long then I may pay Miss Drucker a visit and see what she has to say for herself.'

'I dare say she'll deny it.'

'I dare say she will,' said the inspector. 'By the way, thanks for the tip about the Commercial Street shop. It turns out it was the headquarters of the Carelli gang. We've been trying to close them down for some time now, but with this latest raid we're pretty sure we've got all the ringleaders.'

'Splendid,' said Freddy. By rights he ought to have given the credit to Corky, who had done all the leg-work in finding the place, but naturally he did no such thing. 'Any news on the Kibbles?'

'He's been much more disposed to talk since he found out he's not suspected of murder any more,' said Entwistle. 'He's pretty much admitted everything, but he's already working up his sob-story for the jury. It was all for Birdie's sake, you see. She took up with the cocaine and goodness knows what else besides during the war. He'd been trying to keep her on the straight and narrow for years, but she would keep relapsing, and in the end he was forced to start dealing in it just to make sure she wasn't taking the bad stuff. At least, that's his tale. He still denies giving any of it to Dorothy Dacres, though.'

'Perhaps it wasn't hers,' said Freddy. 'A lot of people were in and out that night. Perhaps someone left it there by mistake. Not I, of course,' he went on hurriedly, at the sight of the inspector's suspicious expression. 'I never touch it myself.'

'Well, there'll be a lot less of it about now we've caught the Carelli gang,' said Entwistle. He stood up and prepared to go out. 'By the way, that friend of yours—the tall one with the teeth. You might try and keep him in check. He's been getting in the way of our officers in the execution of their duty.'

'I only wish I could help, inspector,' said Freddy, 'but he's nothing to do with me. They keep him under lock and key at the *Herald* as a rule, but sometimes he gnaws through his chains and gets out. I suggest you speak to them.'

'Hmm,' said Entwistle, and departed.

'That was quite a story you got, thanks to Mr. Cosgrove,' remarked Sergeant Bird.

'Yes, it was, wasn't it?' said Freddy. 'I don't think he caught my best side, though. A chap never looks at his finest when he's dangling upside-down from a rooftop. Still, trust the police to turn up just in time. I have a gift for many things—or so my mother tells me—but flying isn't one of them.'

He saluted the sergeant and went out. In the street he bumped into Corky Beckwith, who was hovering around with a notebook.

'Ah, Freddy,' he said. 'None the worse for your little adventure of the other day, I see. What a story—and what a stroke of luck for you!'

'I can't say it felt like that at the time,' said Freddy.

'No? I dare say you haven't been in the business long enough. Give it a few more years and I promise you'll lose all sense of fear.'

'And shame, no doubt.'

'Oh, *that*,' said Corky dismissively, with a wave of the hand. 'Still, I've obviously taught you well. It doesn't quite match my triumph at catching the Kibbles single-handedly, but it's not bad, not bad at all. I do believe I shall have to keep an eye on you, or I might have to start looking to my laurels—although I don't think I need worry *just* yet.'

'Rubbish,' said Freddy.

'Nothing of the sort. Remind me to tell you of the time I escaped from a gang of murderous boat-thieves. They were all set to tie me to an anchor and throw me into the sea, but I managed to overpower them using a trick I learned from a chap in Singapore, then jumped overboard and swam to shore. That little story kept me going for weeks, and earned me honorary life membership of the Hunstanton Boat Builders' Association. They still send me their quarterly journal, and I do believe I shall never have to pay for dinner in Norfolk again.' He glanced at his watch. 'Oh, is that the time already? I'll be late if I don't hurry.'

'Where are you going?'

'Bloomsbury,' said Corky. 'I'm due to attend a meeting of the Women's Poetry Society. Terrible things are afoot there, I understand.'

He strode off with a wave, and Freddy headed back towards Fleet Street. Outside the *Clarion* building he saw Gussie Lippincott, who beamed at the sight of him.

'They said you were out, and I thought I'd missed you,' she said. 'I was just coming to say goodbye. Seymour and I are going to America. Dickie Sanders has decided he doesn't want the job at the magazine after all, so Seymour is taking his place. Isn't it simply thrilling?'

Freddy duly gave his congratulations.

'But what shall you do?' he said. 'I'm sorry about *For Every Yesterday*, by the way.'

She sighed.

'Yes, it's all been rather tiresome,' she said. 'They've post-poned it indefinitely. I don't know whether the thing will ever be made now, but I've decided to stop thinking about it. I shall parade myself around the studios and see if I can't get a part or two. Ken is going to put in a good word for me.'

'You're taking it very well.'

'Of course I am,' she said. 'I haven't got the part, but neither has anybody else. But it shall be mine one day, I'm certain of it. I was born to play Helen Harper, and as soon as they decide to start production again I shall be there, demanding they give me the rôle. I won't be thwarted.'

'I suppose this whole mess has left a lot of people disap-pointed,' said Freddy. 'What about Robert Kenrick? This film was a big opportunity for him, too. Is he going to Hollywood?'

'Not yet,' said Gussie. 'A little bird told me the other day that he's got another part practically in the bag here in London. He and Sarah are getting married soon, and she's going to look after the business side of his career. I'm so pleased—he's a darling, and tremendously talented, but he simply hasn't the head for this sort of thing. She'll take care of him and see he doesn't come to harm. You know that Basil had been pushing dope onto him? Sarah will put a stop to all that.'

'I'm glad to hear it,' said Freddy.

'Anyway, I'm so pleased I've caught you,' she said. 'You will look out for me in all the film magazines, won't you? I'm going to be quite disgustingly famous.'

'I have no doubt of it,' he said.

They smiled at one another for a moment.

'Well, goodbye, then,' she said.

She stepped forward and gave him a kiss that was a little more than just friendly.

'I can see Seymour is going to have his hands full with you,' said Freddy, when she stepped back again.

She giggled.

'I know, I'm the most awful flirt,' she said. 'I can't help it. But so are you.'

'Oh, well,' he said. 'There's no harm in a little fun.'

'I agree entirely,' she said. 'And now I simply must run. Seymour wants to take some photographs before we go.'

She squeezed his hand and hurried off. Freddy watched her until she was out of sight, then turned into the *Clarion* building. Lady Featherstone was on the committee of the Women's Poetry Society, he seemed to remember. If there really were terrible things afoot, then he had better speak to Jolliffe, and quickly.

New Releases

If you'd like to receive news of further releases by Clara Benson, you can sign up to my mailing list here.

CLARABENSON.COM/NEWSLETTER

Or follow me on Facebook.

FACEBOOK.COM/CLARABENSONBOOKS

New to Freddy? Read more about him in the Angela Marchmont mysteries.

CLARABENSON.COM/BOOKS

BOOKS IN THIS SERIES

- A Case of Blackmail in Belgravia
- A Case of Murder in Mayfair
- A Case of Conspiracy in Clerkenwell
- A Case of Duplicity in Dorset
- A Case of Suicide in St. James's

ALSO BY CLARA BENSON:
The Angela Marchmont Mysteries

Made in the USA
Monee, IL
10 November 2020